S. R. van Duzer

Market price list of drugs

S. R. van Duzer

Market price list of drugs

ISBN/EAN: 9783742819123

Manufactured in Europe, USA, Canada, Australia, Japa

Cover: Foto ©Andreas Hilbeck / pixelio.de

Manufactured and distributed by brebook publishing software (www.brebook.com)

S. R. van Duzer

Market price list of drugs

S. R. Van Duzer,

Wholesale Druggist,

Importer and Manufacturer,

35 Barclay St. & 40 Park Place,

New-York.

114 & 116 Southampton Row,   37 Boulevard Haussmann,
London.   Paris.

CONTENTS.

✤

"SPECIALTIES."

Of our own Manufacture. Standard Articles.

PAINTS AND COLORS.

Office of S. R. Van Duzer,

New-York, April, 1880.

To the Trade :

I TAKE pleasure in presenting you, herewith, my Catalogue with prices of to-day. It is not offered as a full list. My stock embraces every article in the Drug and other Departments enumerated in this Catalogue. The prices (subject to changes in market values) are net, except where discounts are noted. All inquiries by mail will receive prompt attention, and special quotations given for large quantities and goods in original packages.

÷

Department of Specialties.

The extensive line of articles offered in this Department are all of my own manufacture, bearing my own name and exclusive trade-marks. These articles have for many years had a very large sale with the best and largest houses in the trade. No similar goods of either foreign or domestic manufacture surpass them in quality, and the prices are fixed to meet the closest buyers.

÷

Department of Paints, Colors, &c.

Stock full and complete, each article bearing my own name and exclusive trade-marks. The same high standard qualities will be maintained. Genuine, Royal and Crown brands of Colors, dry and ground in Pure Linseed Oil.

White Lead, Zinc, Varnishes, Brushes, &c., all at lowest manufacturers' prices.

Special quotations, and inquiries by mail promptly answered.

Yours, very respectfully,

S. R. Van Duzer,

35 Barclay Street and 40 Park Place,
New-York.

S. R. VAN DUZER,

MARKET PRICE LIST.

DRUGS.

New-York, April, 1880.

Terms Net Cash, payable within 30 days, in current funds in New-York, subject to draft if not paid at the expiration of that time. **Prices subject to future changes in market.** We give in column two prices ; generally the difference only covers the increased cost of putting up small quantities. Original packages always at the lowest prices.

Acid, Acetic, No. 8	lb.	$ .12	$ .15
" " U. S. P	lb.	.16	.18
" " Glacial, 1 lb. bots	lb.	.55	.60
" Arsenious. Chem. pure	oz.	.10	.12
" Benzoic, English	oz.	.40	.45
" " German	oz.	.22	.25
" Carbolic Crystals,			
Calvert's No. 1, 1 lb. bots.	lb.	1.90	2.00
" " 2, 1 lb. "	lb.	1.30	1.40
" Commercial, 1 lb. bots	lb.	.60	.65
S. R. V. D., 1 lb. bots	lb.	.45	.50
" 1 oz. "	oz.	.06	.08
" Carbolic Solution,			
Calvert's No. 4, 1 lb. bots	lb.	.60	.65
S. R. V. D., 1 lb. bots	doz.	3.50	....
" 1 lb. "	gross.	36.00	....
Crude, 10% bbls.	gall.	.40	.50
" 75% bbls	gall.	1.10	1.35
" Chromic, 1 oz. bots	oz.	.20	.25
" Citric	lb.	.80	.85
" Fluoric, 1 lb. bots	lb.	2.00	2.25
" Gallic, 1 lb. boxes	lb.	1.85	1.90
" " 1 oz. bots	oz.	.18	.20
" Hydrobromic, Conc., 1 lb. bots	lb.	2.00	2.25
" Lactic, Conc., 1 oz. bots	oz.	.26	.30
" " Dilute U. S. P., 1 oz. bots	oz.	.11	.12
" Muriatic, 18°, 6 lb. bots	lb.	.04	.06
" " 18°, by carboy, 120 lbs	lb.	.02½	....
" " Chem. pure, 6 lb. bots	lb.	.25	.28
" " Medicinal, 6 lb. "	lb.	.06	.08
" Nitric, 38°, 7 lb. bots	lb.	.11	.13
" " 38°, by carboy, 120 lbs	lb.	.09	....
" " Chem. pure, 7 lb. bots	lb.	.25	.27
" " Medicinal, 7 lb. "	lb.	.12	.14
" Nitro-Muriatic, 1 lb. bots	lb.	.50	.55
" Oleic, crude, 1 lb. jars	lb.	.40	.45
" " purified, 1 lb. bots	lb.	1.00	1.10
" Oxalic	lb.	.12	.15
" Phosphoric, Diluted,			
1 lb. bots	lb.	.22	.25
Made from Phosphorus, 1 lb. bots	lb.	.30	.35
" Phosphoric, Glacial, 1 lb. bots	lb.	.95	1.00
" " " 1 oz. "	oz.	.09	.10
" Picric, 1 lb. cans	lb.	.60	.65
" Prussic, U. S. P., 1 oz. bots	oz.	.07	.09
" " Scheele's, 1 oz. bots	oz.	.30	.35
" Pyrogallic, 1 oz. bots	oz.	.40	.45
" Pyroligneous, crude	gall.	.25	.30
" Salicylic, White, 1 lb. bots	lb.	2.00	2.25
" " 1 oz. "	oz.	.18	.20
" Sulphuric Aromatic (Elixir Vitriol)	lb.	.50	.55
" " 66°, in 9 lb. bots	lb.	.04	.05
" " 66°, by carboy, 160 lbs	lb.	.02¼	....
" " Chem. pure, 9 lb. bots	lb.	.25	.28
" Tannic, 1 lb. boxes	lb.	2.00	2.10
" " 1 oz. bots	oz.	.15	.18
" Tartaric Crystals	lb.	.56	.58
" " Powdered	lb.	.58	.62

Item	Unit		
Aconitia, ⅛ oz. bots	⅛ oz.	$2.10	$2.20
Alcohol, Absolute	gall.	4 00	4.25
" 95%	gall.	2.20	2.25
" " by bbl	gall.	2.10	....
" Deodorized (Cologne Spirits)	gall.	2.40	2.50
" Wood	gall.	1.40	1.50
" " by bbl	gall.	1.30	....
Allspice	lb.	.16	.18
" Powdered	lb.	.22	.25
" " in cans, S.R.V.D.& Co's (see page 61).			
Almonds, Bitter, shelled	lb.	.42	.45
" Sweet, "	lb.	.38	.40
Alum, Ammonio-Ferric, 1 lb. bots	lb.	.50	.55
" " " 1 oz. "	oz.	.06	.08
" Dried	lb.	.20	.25
" " Powdered	lb.	.25	.30
" Ground	lb.	.04	.05
" " by bbl	lb.	.02½	....
" Lump	lb.	.04	.05
" " by bbl	lb.	.02¼	....
" Powdered	lb.	.08	.10
" " by bbl	lb.	.06½	....
Ammonia, Spirits of, 1 lb. bots	lb.	.40	.45
" " Aromatic, 1 lb. bots	lb.	.45	.50
" Water of, FFF, 16½°	lb.	.07	.09
" " FFFF, 20°	lb.	.10	.12
" "Conc., U.S.P., 26°, 1 lb. bots	lb.	.13	.15
Ammonium, Benzoate, 1 oz. bots	oz.	.50	.55
" Bromide, 1 lb. "	lb.	.52	.55
" Carbonate	lb.	.20	.22
" " in jars, 20 lbs	lb.	.19	....
" Muriate	lb.	.14	.16
" " Granulated	lb.	.18	.20
" " Powdered	lb.	.22	.25
" Sulphate, crude	lb.	.07	.10
" Valerianate, crystals, 1 oz. bots	oz.	.38	.40
Amyl, Nitrite 1 oz. bots	oz.	.35	.40
Aniline, Black (Aniline Salts)	lb.	.60	.65
" " Crystals	lb.	3.00	3.25
" Blue	lb.	3.00	6.00
" Brown	lb.	2.00	2.50
" Green Paste	lb.	3.00	5.00
" " Crystals, extra	lb.	8.00	9.00
" Orange	lb.	2.00	2.25
" Purple	lb.	4.00	8.00
" Pink	lb.	8.00	12.00
" Red	lb.	1.00	1.25
" " Small Crystals, Extra	lb.	2.50	2.75
" Scarlet	lb.	2.00	2.25
" Violet	lb.	5.00	7.00
" Yellow	lb.	5.00	6.00
Aniline Dye Colors, Proprietary (see page 40).			
Annatto	lb.	.35	.38
" by basket, 40 lbs	lb.	.30	....
Anodyne, Hoffman's, 1 lb. bots	lb.	.45	.50
Antimony, Black	lb.	.09	.11
" " Powd., pure	lb.	.12	.15
" Chloride, crystals	lb.	2.00	2.25
" " Solut. (But. of), 1 lb. bots	lb.	.25	.28
" Metallic (Regulus)	lb.	.18	.20
" Oxide, White	lb.	.60	.65
" Oxysulph.(Kerme's Min.), 1 lb. bots	lb.	1.25	1.35
Aqua Fortis, 36°	lb.	.10	.12
" " 36°, by carboy, 120 lbs	lb.	.07½	....
Argols, Red	lb.	.10	.12
" " Powdered	lb.	.12	.15
" White	lb.	.30	.35
Arrowroot, American	lb.	.08	.10
" Bermuda	lb.	.45	.50
" Jamaica	lb.	.25	.30
" " by tin, 14 lbs	lb.	.20	....
" St. Vincent	lb.	.18	.20
" " by tin, 28 lbs	lb.	.15	....
" Taylor's, ¼ lb. foil	lb.	.34	.38
" " ¼ lb. " by box, 12 lbs	lb.	.33	....
" " ½ lb. "	lb.	.34	.38

Arrowroot, Taylor's, ½ lb. foil. by box, 12 lbs.	lb.	$ .33	...
" " 1 lb. tin cans	lb.	.33	$ .37
Arsenic, Iodide, 1 oz. bots	oz.	.66	.70
" White Lump	lb.	.15	.18
" " Powdered, pure	lb.	.22	.25
" " " commercial	lb.	.06	.08
Atropia, ⅛ oz. bots	⅛ oz.	1.60	1.65
" Sulphate, ⅛ oz. bots	⅛ oz.	1.50	1.55
Balsam Copaiva, Angostura	lb.	.75	.80
" " Para	lb.	.75	.80
" " Solidifiable	lb.	.85	.90
" " Solidified, 1 lb. jars	lb.	.95	1.00
" Fir, Canada	gall.	1.65	1.80
" " "	lb.	.35	.40
" Peru, true	lb.	3.25	3.50
" Tolu, "	lb.	.75	.85
" Turlington's	lb.	.75	.85
Bark, Angostura	lb.	.50	.60
" Barberry	lb.	.22	.25
" Bayberry	lb.	.08	.10
" " Powdered	lb.	.15	.18
" Butternut	lb.	.18	.20
" Canella Alba	lb.	.12	.15
" Cascarilla	lb.	.12	.15
" " Powdered	lb.	.20	.25
" Cassia	lb.	.23	.25
" " Powdered	lb.	.32	.35
" " " in cans, S. R. V. D. & Co's (see page 61).			
" " Extra	lb.	.38	.42
" " " Powdered	lb.	.48	.52
" Cinnamon, Ceylon	lb.	1.10	1.20
" " " Powdered	lb.	1.25	1.35
" Cramp	lb.	.25	.28
" Elm, Select	lb.	.15	.18
" " Ground	lb.	.12	.15
" " " ¼ lb. and ½ lb. papers	lb.	.18	.20
" " " 2 oz. papers	lb.	.20	.22
" " Powdered	lb.	.20	.22
" " " 2 oz. papers	lb.	.25	.30
" " " 1 oz. "	lb.	.30	.35
" Hemlock, Ground	lb.	.12	.15
" " Powdered	lb.	.16	.18
" Mezereon	lb.	.20	.25
" Oak, Black (Quercitron)	lb.	.06	.08
" " White, Ground	lb.	.15	.18
" Peruvian, Calisaya	lb.	2.00	2.10
" " " Powdered	lb.	2.15	2.25
" " Pale	lb.	.75	.90
" " " Powdered	lb.	.90	1.05
" " Red	lb.	2.25	2.35
" " " Powdered	lb.	2.40	2.50
" " " Rubingosa	lb.	.50	.60
" " " " Powdered	lb.	.60	.70
" " Yellow	lb.	.18	.20
" " " Powdered	lb.	.25	.30
" Poplar	lb.	.12	.15
" " Ground	lb.	.15	.18
" " Powdered	lb.	.20	.25
" Prickly Ash	lb.	.18	.20
" " " Ground	lb.	.22	.25
" " " Powdered	lb.	.25	.30
" Rhamnus Frangula	lb.	.15	.18
" Sassafras	lb.	.10	.12
" " Powdered	lb.	.18	.25
" Soap Tree (Quillaya)	lb.	.18	.20
" " " Powdered	lb.	.25	.30
" Tamarac	lb.	.25	.28
" Wahoo	lb.	.25	.30
" White Ash	lb.	.22	.25
" Wild Cherry, Extra	lb.	.12	.15
" " " " Ground	lb.	.15	.18
" " " Powdered	lb.	.20	.25
Barley, Pearl	lb.	.05	.07
" " by keg, 100 lbs.	lb.	.04	...
Barium, Chloride (Muriate)	lb.	.15	.18
Baryta, Caustic, Anhydrous, 1 lb. bots	lb.	3.00	3.10

Item	Unit	Price	Price 2
Bath Brick, English, in bbls	per 100.	$3.00	....
" " " in boxes, 2 doz	box.	.75	....
" " Dust, in papers, boxes, 2 doz	box.	1.50	....
Bay Rum, pure imported	gall.	2.50	$2.75
" " " " in bots. S.R.V.D.& Co's (see page 65).			
Beans, Tonca, Angostura	lb.	1.90	2.00
" Vanilla, Prime Mexican	lb.	18.00	19.00
" " Good "	lb.	17.00	18.00
" " Ordinary "	lb.	14.00	15.00
Benzole, Pure, 1 lb. bots	lb.	1.00	1.10
Berries, Cocculus Indicus (Fish Berries)	lb.	.10	.12
" Cubeb	lb.	.20	.22
" " Powdered	lb.	.25	.27
" Juniper, Italian	lb.	.06	.08
" " " Powdered	lb.	.15	.18
" Prickly Ash	lb.	.22	.25
" Sumac	lb.	.13	.16
Bismuth, Citrate and Ammonia Sol'n, 1 lb. bots.	lb.	.40	.45
" Oxychloride, 1 lb. bots	lb.	2.20	2.30
" Subcarbonate, 1 lb. "	lb.	2.65	2.75
" Subnitrate, 1 lb. "	lb.	2.15	2.25
" Tannate, 1 oz. bots.	oz.	.58	.60
Black Drop, 1 lb. bots	lb.	2.00	2.25
Bladders, small	doz.	.50	.60
" med.	doz.	.60	.70
" large	doz.	.90	1.00
Blatta Orientalis (Remedy for Dropsy)	oz.	2.75	3.00
Blue Vitriol (Copper Sulphate)	lb.	.10	.12
" " by bbl	lb.	.09	....
" " Powdered	lb.	.27	.30
Borax, Refined	lb.	.13	.15
" " by case	lb.	.12	....
" " Powdered	lb.	.14	.16
Broma, Baker's	lb.	.44	.47
" " by box, 12 lbs	lb.	.42	....
Bromine, 1 lb. bots	lb.	.60	.65
" 1 oz. "	oz.	.06	.08
Buds, Balm of Gilead	lb.	.38	.40
" Cassia	lb.	.42	.46
Caffein, ⅛ oz. bots	oz.	2.50	2.75
Calcium, Bromide, 1 lb. bots.	lb.	1.25	1.35
" " 1 oz.	oz.	.10	.12
" Chloride, fused, white, 1 lb. bots	lb.	.55	.60
" Hypophosphate, 1 lb. bots	lb.	2.50	2.60
" Lactate, 1 oz. bots	oz.	.25	.28
" Lacto-phosphate, 1 oz. bots	oz.	.40	.45
" Oxalate, 1 oz. bots	oz.	.25	.30
" Sulpho-carbolate, 1 oz. bots	oz.	.18	.20
Camphor, Mono-Bromated, 1 oz. bots	oz.	.40	.45
Candy, Colt's-foot rock, 5 lb. boxes	lb.	.25	.30
" " " 5 lb. " Eng. gen.	lb.	.50	.60
" Gum-Drops, 5 lb. boxes	lb.	.32	.35
" Rock, Red	lb.	.17	.20
" " " on strings, 5 lb. boxes	lb.	.18	.21
" " White	lb.	.17	.20
" " " on strings, 5 lb. boxes	lb.	.18	.21
" " Yellow	lb.	.17	.20
" " " on strings, 5 lb. boxes	lb.	.18	.21
Cantharides, Russian	lb.	1.20	1.25
" " Powdered	lb.	1.40	1.50
Caramel (Liquor-Coloring)	gall.	1.25	1.50
Carbon, Bi-sulphuret, 1 lb. bots	lb.	.24	.27
Carmine, No. 6, 1 oz. bots	oz.	.25	.30
" " 40, 1 " "	oz.	.60	.65
" " 40, 1 lb. "	lb.	7.50	8.00
Castor, Fiber, Russian	lb.	4.25	4.50
Cerate, Cantharides, 1 lb. cans	lb.	1.00	....
" Extract Cantharides, 1 lb. jars	lb.	1.25	....
" Goulard's, 1 lb. jars	lb.	.50	....
" Resin, 1 lb. jars	lb.	.50	....
" " Comp., 1 lb. jars	lb.	.50	....
" Simple, 1 lb. jars	lb.	.50	....
" Turner's, 1 lb "	lb.	.50	....
" Zinc, Carb., true, 1 lb. jars	lb.	.50	....
Cerium, Oxalate, 1 oz.	oz.	.18	.20
Chalk, French Cut	lb.	.12	.15

Chalk, French Powdered ....lb. $ .06 $ .10
"   " White, powdered (Talc)......lb. .10 .12
. "   Precipitated English.................lb. .12 .14
"   Prepared in drops...................lb. .06 .08
"   "   " " by boxes, 25 lbs.....lb. .04 ....
"   Red, in fingers.....................lb. .06 .08
"   " in lumps ....lb. .05 .07
"   White ....lb. .02 .03
"   " by bbl........ ....lb. .00½ ....
Charcoal, Animal, Powdered (Ivory Black) ...lb. .05 .06
"   Ordinary   "   ....lb. .08 .10
"   Willow ....lb. .15 .18
"   " in 1 lb. boxes .... lb. .16 .19
Chinoidine, Purified, 1 oz. rolls............oz. .14 .16
Chloral-hydrate, Am., 1 lb. bots............lb. 1.75 1.85
"   " 1 oz. " ....oz. .16 .18
"   Croton, Am., 1 oz. bots......oz. 1.15 1.25
"   German, 1 lb. bots..........lb. 1.65 1.75
"   " ½ lb. " ....lb. 1.80 1.90
"   " ¼ lb. " ....lb. 2.00 2.10
"   " 1 oz. " ....lb. 3.10 3.20
"   Crystals, 1 lb. bots...lb. 1.75 1.85
"   " ½ lb. " ...lb. 1.90 2.00
"   " ¼ lb. " ....lb. 2.10 2.20
"   " 1 oz. " ...lb. 3.25 3.35
"   Schering's, 1 lb. bots.lb. 1.85 1.90
"   " ½ lb. " .lb. 2.00 2.10
"   " ¼ lb. " .lb. 2.25 2.50
"   " 1 oz. " .lb. 3.25 3.50
"   " Crys., 1 lb.bots.lb. 2.00 2.10
"   " " ½ lb. " .lb. 2.15 2.25
"   " " ¼ lb. " .lb. 2.35 2.40
"   " " 1 oz. " .lb. 3.40 3.50
Chloroform ....lb. 1.00 1.05
"   Purified, 1 lb. bots..............lb. 1.30 1.35
Chocolate, Baker's Premium, boxes 12, 25 lbs.lb. .34 .36
"   " German Sweet, 6 and 12 lbs.lb. .22 .24
Cinchona, Alkaloid, Pure, 1 oz. bots ....oz. .45 .50
"   Muriate, 1 oz. bots...............oz. 1.00 1.10
"   Sulphate, 1 oz. " .... oz. .30 .35
"   Mixture, 3 oz. boxes............box. .40 ....
Cinchonidia, Pure, Alkaloid, 1 oz. bots.......oz. 1.50 1.60
"   Sulphate, 1 oz.....................oz. 1.15 1.20
Cincho-Quinine, 1 oz. bots........ ....oz. 1.60 1.70
Citron ....lb. .22 .25
Clay, China.... .... lb. .05 .07
"   Pipe ....lb. .04 .06
"   " Powdered......................lb. .10 .12
"   Potter's ....lb. .05 .08
Cloves ....lb. .38 .40
"   Powdered.........................lb. .45 .48
"   In cans, S. R. V. D. & Co's (see page 61).
Cobalt.... ... .lb. .19 .20
"   Powdered.. ....lb. .25 .30
Cochineal, Honduras......................lb. .90 .95
"   " Powdered..............lb. 1.05 1.10
Cocoa, Baker's, Pure, boxes 12 and 30 lbs ....lb. .37 .39
"   Taylor's Homœ ....:....lb. .35 .37
"   Butter.. .... lb. .45 .50
Cocoanut, Desiccated, 1 lb. packages........lb. .26 .25
"   " ½ lb. " ....lb. .27 .26
"   " Assorted " ....lb. .26 .25
Codeia, ⅛ oz. bots.......... ....oz. 3.75 4.00
Collodion, 1 lb. bots.....................lb. .90 1.00
"   1 oz. " ....doz. 2.00 2.25
"   Cantharidal, 1 lb. bots ....lb. 2.75 3.00
"   " 1 oz. bots.......... doz. 2.75 3.00
Colocynth Apples, select................lb. .50 .55
"   " Powdered .... lb. .60 .65
Confection, Rose, 1 lb. jars..............lb. .40 ....
"   Senna, 1 lb. " ....lb. .40 ....
Copperas ....lb. .02½ .03
"   by bbl.......................lb. .01¼ ....
Corks (see page 30).
Cowhage Down, 1 oz. cans...... ....oz. .45 .50
Cream Tartar Crystals................ ......lb. .38 .39

Cream Tartar, Powdered	lb.	$	.39	$ .41
" " " by box, 50 lbs	lb.		.38	....
Creosote, Commercial, 1 lb. bots	lb.		.65	.70
" " from Wood, 1 lb. bots	lb.		3.00	3.25
Crocus Martis	lb.		.12	.15
" Metallorum	lb.		.35	.40
Cudbear	lb.		.25	.28
Dextrin	lb.		.14	.16
Dextro-Quinine, 1 oz. bots	oz.		1.50	1.55
Dragon's Blood			.50	.55
" " Powdered			.65	.75
Earth, Fuller's	lb.		.04	.06
" " Powdered	lb.		.10	.12
Emery Flour	lb.		.06	.08
" various sizes, grain	lb.		.07	.10
Ergot	lb.		.70	.75
" Powdered	lb.		.80	.85
Essences, S. R. V. D. & Co's (see page 35).				
Ess. Jamaica Ginger, S.R.V.D. & Co's (see page 57).				
" " " "Rolands" (see page 59).				
Ether, Acetic, 1 lb. bots	lb.		.82	.85
" Chloric, 1 lb. "	lb.		.78	.80
" Sulphuric, 1 lb. bots	lb.		.62	.65
" " Conc., 1 lb. bots	lb.		.68	.71
" " Washed, 1 lb. bots	lb.		.65	.68
EXTRACTS, FLAVORING, S. R. V. D. & Co's				
Fruit Brand, Standard Quality (see page 51).				
EXTRACTS, FLAVORING, "Lupin's" (see page 53).				
" " "Roland's" (see page 55).				
EXTRACTS, FLUID, S.R.V.D.& Co's (see page 24).				
EXTRACTS, SOLID, S.R.V.D.& Co's (see page 26).				
EXTRACTS, PERFUMERY, "Lautier Fils,"				
in pint and half pint bottles, glass stoppers.				
Bouq. de Caroline, Night-Blooming Cereus	lb.		3.00	3.25
Ess. Bouquet, Orange	lb.		3.00	3.25
Frangipanni, Patchouly	lb.		3.00	3.25
Heliotrope, Pond Lily	lb.		3.00	3.25
Jasmin, Rose	lb.		3.00	3.25
Jockey Club, Rose Geranium	lb.		3.00	3.25
Magnolia, Stephanotis	lb.		3.00	3.25
Marechale, Tea Rose	lb.		3.00	3.25
Mignonette, Tuberose	lb.		3.00	3.25
Millefleur, Upper Ten	lb.		3.00	3.25
Moss Rose, Violet	lb.		3.00	3.25
Musk, West End	lb.		3.00	3.25
Musk Rose, White Rose	lb.		3.00	3.25
New-Mown Hay, Ylang Ylang	lb.		3.00	3.25
Extract Logwood, bulk boxes, 12, 24, 48 lb.	lb.		.10	.11
" " 1 lb. packages, bxs., 24 lb.	lb.		.12	.13
" " ¼ lb. " " 24 lb.	lb.		.13	.14
" " ½ lb. " " 24 lb.	lb.		.15	.16
" " Assort'd " " 24 lb.	lb.		.14	.15
Eye Stones	doz.		.50	.60
Fish Sounds	lb.		1.25	1.50
Flour, Rice, bulk	lb.		.10	.12
" " 1 lb. papers	lb.		.12	.14
Flowers, Arnica	lb.		.17	.20
" " Powdered	lb.		.30	.35
" Borage	lb.		.70	.75
" Calendula (Marigold)	lb.		.50	.60
" Chamomile, Belgian, new crop	lb.		.33	.38
" " German, " "	lb.		.35	.40
" " Roman, " "	lb.		.35	.40
" Elder	lb.		.18	.20
" Koosso, true	lb.		.65	.75
" " Powdered	lb.		.75	.90
" Lavender	lb.		.10	.12
" Poppy, Red	lb.		.55	.60
" Rose, Pale	lb.		.60	.65
" " Red	lb.		.75	.85
" " Powdered	lb.		.90	1.00
" Rosemary	lb.		.40	.50
" Saffron, American	lb.		.55	.60
" " Spanish, true, Valencia	lb.		12.50	13.00
" Tilia, with leaves	lb.		.25	.30
" " without leaves	lb.		.60	.65

Flowers, Violet	lb.	$ .70	$ .75
Garlics	string.	.18	.20
Gelatine, Cooper's, sheet	lb.	.90	.95
" " sheet, by box, 12 lbs	lb.	.85	....
" " shred	lb.	.90	.95
" " " by box, 12 lbs	lb.	.85	....
" " " 2 oz. pps	lb.	.90	.95
" " " 2 oz.pps.,by box,12 lbs.	lb.	.85	....
" Cox's	doz.	1.55	1.65
" "	gross.	18.50	...:
" French, Pink, sheets	lb.	1.10	1.20
" " White, Gold Label	lb.	.70	.75
" " " Silver "	lb.	.60	.65
" " " Copper "	lb.	.50	.55
Glue, A	lb.	.14	.16
" AA	lb.	.18	.20
" AAA	lb.	.25	.27
" Cooper's, A Extra, bbl. or less, 85 lbs.	lb.	.32	.35
" " No. 1, Ex., " " 85 lbs.	lb.	.28	.30
" " " 1, " " 85 lbs.	lb.	.24	.26
" " " IX, " " 100 lbs.	lb.	.20	.22
" " " 1¼, " " 100 lbs.	lb.	.17	.19
" " " 1⅜, " " 110 lbs.	lb.	.16	.18
" " " 1½, " " 130 lbs.	lb.	.15	.17
" " " 1⅝, " " 135 lbs.	lb.	.13	.15
" " " 1¾, " " 150 lbs.	lb.	.12	.14
" " " 2, " " 150 lbs.	lb.	.11	.13
" " " 2⅛, " " 165 lbs.	lb.		
" " " 2¼, " " 165 lbs.	lb.		
" " " 2⅜, " " 165 lbs.	lb.		
Less 5% in quantities by the bbl.			
" Frozen	lb.	.25	.30
Glycerine, S. R. V. D. & Co's, 1 lb. bots	lb.	.35	.40
" S. R. V. D. & Co's. 2 oz. "	doz.	1.00	....
" S. R. V. D. & Co's, bulk	lb.	.23	.28
" S. R. V. D. & Co's, by can, 50 lbs.	lb.	.20	....
Gold, Chloride, 15 gr. bots	doz.	5.30	....
" Leaf, Extra Deep, packs, 20 books	pack.	7.25	7.50
" " Pale, " 20 "	pack.	6.50	6.75
" " Usual, " 20 "	pack.	6.75	7.00
Goulard's Extract, 1 lb. bots	lb.	.20	.25
Grains Paradise	lb.	.15	.18
Guarana (Paulinia)	lb.	1.25	1.35
" Powdered	lb.	1.50	1.60
Gum Aloes, Barbadoes	lb.	.28	.30
" " " Powdered	lb.	.38	.40
" " Cape	lb.	.15	.18
" " " Powdered	lb.	.25	.28
" " Socotrine, true	lb.	.50	.60
" " " " Powdered	lb.	.65	.75
" Ammoniac, Mass.	lb.	.30	.40
" " Tears	lb.	.45	.50
" " Powdered	lb.	.75	.90
" Arabic, Turkey, extra select	lb.	.45	.50
" " " 1st "	lb.	.40	.45
" " " 2d "	lb.	.35	.40
" " " 3d "	lb.	.30	.35
" " " 4th "	lb.	.25	.30
" " " Sifted Sorts	lb.	.20	.25
" " " Powdered, 1st	lb.	.50	.55
" " " " 2d	lb.	.40	.45
" Assafœtida	lb.	.25	.30
" " Powdered	lb.	.45	.50
" Asphaltum	lb.	.10	.12
" Benzoin, Marbled	lb.	.50	.60
" " Powdered	lb.	.65	.70
" Camphor, Refined	lb.	.32	.35
" " " cakes, case 100 lbs.	lb.	.32	....
" Catechu, Black (Cutch)	lb.	.12	.14
" " " Powdered	lb.	.25	.30
" " Brown (Terra Japon. or Gambier).	lb.	.07	.09
" " " by bale, 150 lbs	lb.	.04¾	....
" " Refined, 1 lb. pack., boxes, 24 lbs.	lb.	.12	.14
" Copal	lb.	.40	.45
" Damar	lb.	.35	.40
" Euphorbium	lb.	.18	.20

Gum Euphorbium, Powdered	lb.	$ .35	$ .40
" Galbanum, "	lb.	1.50	1.60
" " Strained	lb.	.90	1.00
" " Tears	lb.	.75	.85
" Gamboge	lb.	.70	.75
" " Powdered	lb.	.90	.95
" Guaiac	lb.	.40	.45
" " Powdered	lb.	.50	.60
" Kino, true	lb.	.40	.45
" " Powdered	lb.	.50	.55
" Mastic	lb.	1.65	1.75
" " Powdered	lb.	2.00	2.25
" Myrrh, Turkey	lb.	.38	.45
" " " Powdered	lb.	.45	.55
" Olibanum	lb.	.18	.20
" " Tears	lb.	.30	.35
" " Powdered	lb.	.45	.50
" Opium, Turkey	lb.		
" " " Powdered	lb.		
" Sandarac	lb.	.30	.35
" Scammony, Aleppo	lb.	6.00	6.50
" " " Powdered	lb.	7.00	7.50
" Shellac, Bleached	lb.	.50	.55
" " Campbell's	lb.	.50	.55
" " English, No. 1	lb.	.45	.50
" " " " 2	lb.	.40	.45
" " " Powdered	lb.	.65	.70
" Tragacanth, Flake, Aleppo, Natural	lb.	.75	.80
" " " White	lb.	1.00	1.10
" " " " Extra	lb.	1.20	1.25
" " " " Ribbons	lb.	1.40	1.50
" " " Sorts	lb.	.30	.35
" Powdered, Extra	lb.	1.40	1.50
Honey, Strained	lb.	.16	.20
Hops, Loose, Fresh	lb.	.45	.55
" Pressed, 1 lb., ½ lb., and ¼ lb. papers	lb.	.35	.45
Indigo, Bengal	lb.	1.75	1.85
" Caracas	lb.	1.20	1.25
" Compound (Sulphate)	lb.	.60	.65
" Madras	lb.	1.00	1.10
" Manila, Extra	lb.	1.10	1.15
" " A	lb.	1.00	1.05
Iodine, Resublimed, 1 lb. bots	lb.	6.40	6.50
" " 1 oz. "	oz.	.44	.47
Iodoform, 1 oz. "	oz.	.95	1.00
Iron, Carb., Precipitated	lb.	.19	.22
" " Proto. (Vallet's Mass)	lb.	.40	.45
" Chloride, 1 lb. bots	lb.	.65	.75
" " 1 oz. "	oz.	.06	.08
" " Solution for tincture, 1 pt. bots	pt.	.22	.25
" " Tincture	lb.	.32	.35
" Citrate, U. S. P., 1 lb. bots	lb.	.91	.96
" " " 1 oz. "	oz.	.08	.10
" " and Amm. (soluble), 1 lb. bots	lb.	.89	.92
" " " " " 1 oz. "	oz.	.08	.10
" " " Quinine, 1 lb. "	lb.	9.00	9.50
" " " 1 oz. "	oz.	.60	.65
" " " " with Strych. 1 oz. bots	oz.	.70	.75
" " " Strychnine, 1 oz. bots	oz.	.20	.25
" Dialysed, true, Solution, 1 lb. bots	lb.	.90	1.00
" " " "	doz.	7.20	8.00
" Filings	lb.	.10	.12
" Iodide, 1 oz. bots	oz.	.45	.50
" " Syrup of, 1 lb. bots	lb.	.67	.70
" " Tasteless, 1 oz "	oz.	.70	.75
" " " Syrup of, 1 lb. bots	lb.	.75	.85
" Oxide, Black, 1 lb. bots	lb.	.40	.45
" Pyrophosphate, 1 lb. bots	lb.	.88	.90
" " 1 oz. "	oz.	.08	.10
" Quevennes (by Hydrogen), 1 lb. bots	lb.	1.10	1.20
" " " 1 oz. "	oz.	.10	.12
" Sesquichloride, 1 lb. bots	lb.	.70	.75
" " 1 oz. "	oz.	.06	.08
" " Solution, 1 lb. bots	pint.	.22	.25
" Subsulphate, (Monsel's Powd.) 1 lb. bots	lb.	.55	.60
" " " " 1 oz. "	oz.	.05	.07

Iron, Subsulph. Solution (Monsel's), 1 lb.bots.	lb.	$ .30	$ .33
" Sulphate, Pure Crystals............ ....lb.		.06	.08
" " " Dried, 1 lb. bots........lb.		.18	.20
" Sulpho-Carbolate, 1 oz. bots...... ....oz.		.16	.20
" Sulphuret............................lb.		.23	.25
" Tartrate and Ammonia, 1 lb. bots.......lb.		.65	.70
" " " " 1 oz. " ......oz.		.08	.10
" " " Potassium Plates, 1 lb. bots.lb.		.60	.65
" " " " Powdered,1 lb. " lb.		.55	.60
" Valeriante, ⅛ oz., ¼ oz., and 1 oz. bots oz.		.40	.45
Isinglass, American (Fish Glue)... ....lb.		1.85	1.95
" Brazil, Shred ....lb.		3.00	3.25
" Russia, true, Beluga..... ....lb.		3.50	3.75
JUICES, FRUIT, Pure.			
Catawba, quart champ. bots...........doz.		8.00	....
Pine-apple, " " " ....doz.		8.00	....
Raspberry, " " " ....doz.		8.00	....
Strawberry, " " " ....doz.		8.00	....
Kameela, Powdered, 1 oz. bots.............oz.		.12	.15
Lac Dye, Powdered.....................lb.		.35	.40
Lamp Black (see page 84).			
Lapis Calaminaris ....lb.		.08	.10
Lard, Benzoated....................... ...lb.		.30	.35
" Prepared............................lb.		.30	.35
Laudanum......... ... .lb.		1.00	1.10
" in Bottles (see page 35).			
Lead, Acetate (Sugar of), Brown............lb.		.12	.15
" " " White ....lb.		.16	.18
" " " " Powdered...lb.		.28	.30
" Black, Am................... ......lb.		.04	.06
" " E. I ....lb.		.07	.09
" " " Powdered................lb.		.08	.10
" " German ....lb.		.06	.08
" " " Powdered............lb.		.08	.10
" Carbonate (White Lead)............lb.		.08½	.10
" Nitrate.....................lb.		.15	.18
" " Pure, 1 lb. bots...... ....lb.		.50	.60
" Red ....lb.		.07¾	.10
Leaves, Aconite, German....................lb.		.15	.20
" " " Powdered..........lb.		.25	.30
" Belladonna, German................lb.		.22	.25
" " " Powdered ......lb.		.30	.35
" Buchu, Long.......................lb.		.55	.65
" " " Powdered..............lb.		.45	.55
" " Short...... ....lb.		.12	.14
" " " Powdered ....lb.		.20	.25
" Cherry Laurel....................lb.		.60	.65
" Cocoa ....lb.		.50	.60
" Conium, German.... ....lb.		.15	.20
" " " Powdered..... ....lb.		.25	.30
" Digitalis, German................lb.		.15	.20
" " " Powdered..........lb.		.25	.30
" Eucalyptus ....lb.		.20	.25
" Hyoscyamus, German. .. ..lb.		.20	.25
" " " Powdered......lb.		.30	.35
" Jaborandi....... ....lb.		.40	.45
" Laurel, true (Bay Leaves)..... ....lb.		.10	.12
" Matico ... .lb.		.38	.40
" Rosemary ....lb.		.10	.12
" Sage, American................ .lb.		.15	.20
" " Italian. .....,......lb.		.10	.12
" " Powdered...... ....lb.		.15	.18
" " " ¼ tins.............doz.		.60	.70
" Savin.............................lb.		.08	.10
" " Powdered ....lb.		.18	.25
" Senna, Alexandria, Natural....... ...lb.		.18	.20
" " " Sifted............lb.		.30	.35
" " " " extra........lb.		.45	.50
" " " Powdered.......lb.		.30	.40
" " E. I.....................lb.		.12	.15
" " " Powdered..........lb.		.25	.30
" " Tinnively ....lb.		.18	.25
" Stramonium.... ....lb.		.18	.20
" " Powdered...............lb.		.25	.30
" Thyme ....lb.		.18	.20
" " Powdered ....lb.		.20	.25

				$	$
Leaves, Thyme, Powdered, ¼ lb. tins ......doz.				.75	.85
" Uva Ursi..........................lb.				.10	.12
" " Powdered..............lb.				.20	.25
Leeches, Swedish .... per 100				5.50	6.00
Lemon Peel................................lb.				.18	.20
Licorice, Calabria, Corigliano, 16 sticks to lb..lb.				.38	.43
" " " 8 " " ..lb.				.38	.43
" " " 6 " " ..lb.				.38	.43
" " " 4 " " ..lb.				.38	.43
" " Guzzolini, 12½ " " ..lb.				.32	.37
" " " 8 " " ..lb.				.33	.38
" " P. & S., 14½ " " ..lb.				.34	.39
" " P. Di Gerace, 16 " " ..lb.				.32	.37
" " " 8 " " ..lb.				.32	.37
" " " 6 " " ..lb.				.32	.37
" " " 4 " " ..lb.				.32	.37
" " Powdered... ....lb.				.45	.50
" " Ringed....................lb.				.15	.18
" " Sicily, Am............... lb.				.18	.20
" " Scudder's, 6,9 & 15 sticks to lb.lh.				.27	.30
" " Mass... ....lb.				.20	.28
Lime, Carbolate, boxes, 10 lbs.............box.				1.25	....
" " 1 lb............doz.				1.50	....
" Chloride.......... ....lb.				.04	.06
" " 1 lb. bxs, by case 50 lb. 20% dis.lb.				.09	.10
" " ½ lb. " " 50 " 20 " lb.				.10	.11
" " ¼ lb. " " 50 " 20 " lb.				.11	.12
" " Assorted boxes, 50 " 20 " lb.				.10	.11
" Sulphite, 1 lb. bots.................lb.				.25	.27
" " 5 oz. cartons ....doz.				1.35	1.50
Litharge...........................lh.				.07¾	.10
Lozenges, Chloride Potassa, 2 gr...........lb.				.50	....
Also, a full line medicated.					
Lunar Caustic, pure................. ... .oz.				.81	.84
" " No. 2, 67% ....oz.				.57	.60
Lupulin .....,.......................lb.				.45	.55
Lycopodium ....lb.				.50	.55
Lye, concentrated, Pa. Salt Co., boxes 48 lbs.box.				3.75	4.00
" " Greenwich, " 48 lbs.box.				3.75	4.00
Mace ....lb.				.85	.90
" Ground...............................lb.				.95	1.05
" in cans, S. R. V. D. & Co's (see page 61).					
Madder, Dutch ....lb.				.12	.14
Magnesia, Calcined, American, boxes, 12 lbs..lb.				.35	.45
" " " Heavy, 1 lb. bots.lb.				1.50	1.60
" " Eng., Jennings', tins, 12 lbs.lb.				.75	....
" " " " bots, 1 lb .lb.				1.10	1.15
" " Carbonate, Jennings', 2 oz. papers..lb.				.35	.37
" " " 4 oz. " ..lb.				.33	.35
" " " small square.lb.				.65	.68
" " English, 2 oz. papers .lb.				.23	.26
" " " 4 oz. " ..lb.				.23	.26
" " " small square.lb.				.55	.60
" Citrate Solution, S. R.V.D.& Co's.doz.				2.00	....
Magnesium, Metallic, Ribbon.............oz.				3.75	4.50
" " Wire.................oz.				3.75	4.50
Manganese, Black Oxide, Powdered.........lb.				.06	.08
" " " by bbl.... ...lh.				.04½	....
Manna, Flake, large......................lb.				.80	.90
" " small ....lb.				.40	.45
Marble Dust, in bbls......................bbl.				1.25	....
Mercury...............................lb.				.50	.60
" Ammoniated (White Precipitate)....lb.				.84	.88
" Bichloride (Corrosive Sublimate)....lb.				.54	.58
" Biniodide (Red Iodide), 1 oz. bots...oz.				.42	.45
" Bisulphuret (Cinnabar)....... ....lb.				1.25	1.30
" Black Oxide, 1 oz. bots...........oz.				.30	.35
" Bromide, 1 oz. bots.............. oz.				.40	.45
" Cyanide, 1 oz. " ....oz.				.40	.45
" Distilled ....lb.				.65	.70
" Nitrate Crystals, 1 oz. bots.........oz.				.25	.30
" " Solution, 1 oz. " ....oz.				.15	.20
" Oxide, Red (Red Precipitate).......lb.				.74	.78
" " Yellow, German, 1 oz. bots.oz.				.25	.30
" Protiodide (Green Iodide), 1 oz. bots.oz.				.40	.42
" Sub-chloride (Calomel), Am. 1 lb. bots .lb.				.64	.68

Mercury, Sub-chloride (Calomel), Eng. 1 lb.bots.lb.	$1.10	$1.20	
" Subsulphate (Turpeth Mineral).... lb.	1.10	1.15	
" Sulphuret, Black (Ethiops Mineral)..lb.	.78	.83	
" with Chalk, 1 lb. bots............lb.	.41	.43	
" with Magnesia, 1 lb. bots.........lb.	1.15	1.25	
Morphine, Acetate, ½ oz. bots.............oz.			
" Muriate, ⅛ oz. " ....oz.			
" Sulphate, P. & W., 1 oz. bots.....oz.			
" " " ⅛ oz. bots.... oz.			
Moss, Iceland...............................lb.	.10	.12	
" Irish ....lb.	.08	.10	
Musk, Chinese, 1 oz. tins... ....oz.	.50	.55	
" Tonquin, in pods..................oz.	9.50	10.00	
" Tonquin, in grain..................oz.	25.00	26.00	
Mustard, English, "Queen," 18 lb. kegs.......lb.	.33	.35	
" " 10 lb. cans .. ...lb.	.35	.37	
" " 1 lb. " .....doz.	5.50	5.75	
" " ½ lb. " .....doz.	2.75	2.90	
" " ¼ lb. " .... doz.	1.50	1.60	
" " Colman's Durham, 18 lb. kegs..lb.	.31	.33	
" " " 4, 6, 10 lb. cans.lb.	.33	.35	
" " " " ¼ lb. " doz.	1.15	1.25	
" " " D. S. F., 1 lb. " . ..doz.	5.75	6.00	
" " " " ½ lb. " ....doz.	2.90	3.00	
" " " " ¼ lb. " ....doz.	1.60	1.70	
Nutgalls ....lb.	.28	.30	
" Ground ....lb.	.30	.32	
" Powdered ....lb.	.35	.38	
Nutmegs, No. 1, Selected ....lb.	.90	.95	
" Ground ....lb.	1.00	1.10	
" in cans, S. R. V. D. & Co's, (see p. 61).			
Nuts, Areca................................lb.	.50	.60	
Nux Vomica................................lb.	.10	.12	
" " Powdered................lb.	.25	.30	
Oakum ....lb.	.12	.15	
Oatmeal, "Ulster,"........................lb.	.05	.06	
" " by bbl..... ....bbl.	7.75	....	
" " Connaught,"...............bbl.	7.25	....	
" Watergate Mills, bbl. 200 lbs......bbl.	13.50	...	
" " " cases,10, 14 lb. tins, case	12.50	....	
" Robinson's 1 lb. pckgs 30 lb. case..lb.	.08	....	
Oil Almonds, Bitter, Allen's, 1 lb. bots.......lb.	7.25	7.75	
" " Sweet, Allen's................lb.	.63	.68	
" " " French ....lb.	.45	.50	
" Amber, Crude .... lb.	.30	.35	
" Rectified ....lb.	.45	.50	
" Aniseed........................lb.	2.25	2.50	
" Bay Leaves, true............. ... ...lb.	.75	.90	
" Bergamot, Finest ....lb.	3.25	3.50	
" Cade...........................lb.	.30	.40	
" Cajeput ....lb.	1.00	1.25	
" Camphor ....lb.	1.50	1.60	
" Camphorated ....lb.	.70	.75	
" Caraway .... lb.	1.25	1.50	
" " Seed....................lb.	2.25	2.50	
" Cassia .... lb.	1.40	1.50	
" Castor, American, prime white.......lb.	.12½	.13	
" " " in cases, prime white..lb.	.11½	....	
" " " Shaded (Lubricating)..lb.	.11½	.12	
" " S. R. V. D. & Co's, in bots. (see page 35).			
" Cedar, pure.....................lb.	.75	.85	
" Cinnamon, true ... .oz.	2.25	2.50	
" Citronella, Native..................lb.	1.55	1.65	
" " Winter's..............lb.	1.75	1.85	
" Cloves .... lb.	2.40	2.50	
" Cod Liver, Brown, Bergen............gall.	1.00	1.10	
" " " Newfoundland ....gall.	.90	1.00	
" " White, " ....gall.	1.00	1.10	
" " " Norwegian.......gall.	1.35	1.50	
" " S. R. V. D. & Co's, bots. (see page 70).			
" Copaiva.........................lb.	1.30	1.40	
" Cotton Seed.....................gall.	.60	.65	
" " by bbl.................gall.	.56	....	
" Croton, English..................lb.	1.90	2.00	
" Cubeb ....lb.	2.35	2.45	
" Cumin .... lb.	5.50	6.00	

Oil	Erigeron	lb.	$1.65	$1.75
"	Fennel Seed	lb.	1.65	1.75
"	Fireweed	lb.	1.50	1.75
"	Geranium, Rose, French	lb.	16.50	17.50
"	" " Turkish	lb.	8.50	9.00
"	" " Best	lb.	16.00	16.50
"	Hemlock, pure	lb.	.65	.75
"	Juniper Berries	lb.	2.00	2.25
"	" Wood	lb.	.60	.65
"	**Lard**	**gall.**	**.70**	**.75**
"	" by bbl	gall.	.65	....
"	Lavender, Flowers, French	lb.	2.25	2.50
"	" Garden, French, Pure	lb.	1.60	1.75
"	" " Fine	lb.	1.25	1.35
"	Lemon, Finest	lb.	3.50	3.75
"	" Grass, Native	lb.	1.60	1.70
"	" " Winter's	lb.	1.90	2.00
"	**Linseed, Boiled**	**gall.**	**.88**	**.89**
"	" " by bbl	gall.	.86	....
"	" **Raw**	**gall.**	**.83**	**.84**
"	" " by bbl	gall.	.81	....
"	**Machine, Extra**	**gall.**	**.70**	**.75**
"	" " by bbl	gall.	.65	....
"	" No. 1	gall.	.45	.50
"	" No. 1, by bbl	gall.	.40	....
"	Musk, Alcoholic	oz.	.75	1.00
"	Mustard, Essential	oz.	1.00	1.25
"	Mustard, Expressed	gall.	.80	.90
"	Myrbane	lb.	.45	.50
"	**Neatsfoot, Extra**	**gall.**	**.85**	**.90**
"	" " by bbl	gall.	.75	....
"	" **Cooper's**	**gall.**	**1.05**	**1.10**
"	" " by bbl	gall.	.95	....
"	Neroli, Bigarade	oz.	3.50	3.75
"	" Petit Grain	oz.	1.00	1.25
"	**Olive, Pure Malaga**	**gall.**	**1.20**	**1.30**
"	" " In bottles (see page 35).			
"	" " Sublime, Lucca	gall.	3.00	3.25
"	" " " 3 gall. cans (4 can cases)	gall.	2.85	
"	" " Subl., Luc., qts., cases, 1 doz.	case.	7.50	
"	" " " " pints, " 2 doz.	case.	8.50	
"	" " " " ½ pts, " 2 doz.	case.	5.00	
"	" " Callisto, Francesconi & Co's., our own importation, packed expressly for us.			
"	" Marseilles, qts. boxes, 1 doz.	box.	4.00	....
"	" " pts. " 2 "	box.	5.00	....
"	Orange, Bitter	lb.	4.50	4.75
"	" Sweet	lb.	3.25	3.50
"	Orignum, Pure	lb.	.75	.80
"	" Super	lb.	.60	.70
"	" Commercial	lb.	.40	.50
"	Palm, 5 lb. jars	lb.	.20	....
"	Paraffine	gall.	.35	.40
"	" by bbl	gall.	.26	....
"	Pennyroyal	lb.	1.50	1.60
"	Peppermint	lb.	3.00	3.25
"	" Hotchkiss', H. G., bots., 21 oz.	lb.	3.60	3.75
"	Rhodium	oz.	.50	.60
"	Rose, Kissanlik	oz.	6.50	6.75
"	Rosemary, Flowers, French, Eperlé	lb.	1.50	1.75
"	" " No. 1	lb.	1.25	1.50
"	" Trieste	lb.	.55	.65
"	Salad, Union Oil Co.'s	gall.	.60	.65
"	" " " by bbl	gall.	.56	....
"	Sandal Wood, English	lb.	8.00	9.00
"	" " German	lb.	6.50	7.00
"	Sassafras	lb.	.50	.55
"	Savin	lb.	1.25	1.50
"	Seneka	gall.	.70	.80
"	Sesame (Benne)	gall.	1.30	1.40
"	Spearmint	lb.	2.75	3.00
"	**Sperm**	**gall.**	**1.30**	**1.35**
"	" by bbl	gall.	1.25	....
"	" Ex. Bleached (for Sew'g Mach)	gall.	1.50	....

Oil, Sewing Machine, in bots., S.R.V.D.& Co's (see page 69).

" Spike	lb.	$ .30	$ .35
" Spruce	lb.	.40	.35
" **Tanner's**	gall.	.52	.57
" " by bbl.	gall.	.47	....
" Tansy	lb.	3.25	3.50
" Tar	gall.	.45	.50
" Verbena	oz.	1.00	1.25
" **Whale**	gall.	.70	.75
" " by bbl.	gall.	.65	....
" Wintergreen	lb.	3.75	4.00
" Wormseed	lb.	2.00	2.25
" Wormwood	lb.	3.65	3.75
Ointment, Citrine (Nit. Mercury), 1 lb. jars.	lb.	.45	.50
" Mercurial, ½ " 1 lb. "	lb.	.50	.53
" " ⅓ " 1 lb. "	lb.	.42	.45
" Tar 1 lb. jars	lb.	.40	....
" Zinc Oxide, 1 lb. jars	lb.	.60	....
Orange Peel	lb.	.10	.12
" " Ground	lb.	.12	.15
" " Powdered	lb.	.20	.25
Paraffine, Refined	lb.	.22	.25
Paregoric	lb.	.45	.50
" in bottles (see page 37).			
Pearlash (Carbonate Potassium)	lb.	.12	.15
Pepper, Black	lb.	.16	.18
" " Powdered	lb.	.20	.25
" " in cans, S. R.V. D. & Co. (see page 61).			
" Red (Capsicum)	lb.	.20	.25
" " Powdered	lb.	.25	.30
" " " in cans, S.R.V.D. & Co. (see page 61).			
" White	lb.	.25	.30
" " Powdered	lb.	.30	.35
" " " in cans, S. R.V.D.& Co.(see page 61).			
Phosphorus, 1 lb. cans	lb.	1.10	
" 1 oz. "	lb.	.30	.35
Picra, Hiera	lb.	.30	.35
Pill, Blue, 1 lb. jars	lb.	.43	.48
" " Powdered, 1 lb. bots	lb.	.68	.73
Pitch, Burgundy, American, boxes 10 & 20 lbs.	lb.	.06	.08
" " True	lb.	.10	.12
Plaster,Adh.,Spd., Am.,Davidson's, 5 yd. rolls.	yd.	.15	....
" " " " Ellis, 5 yd. " yd.		.15	....
" " " " " 1 yd. " doz.		1.75	....
" " " English, 5 yd. " yd.		.16	....
" " " " 1 yd. " doz.		2.25	....
Plaster Paris, by bbl.	bbl.	1.25	....
" " Dentists', by bbl.	bbl.	1.50	....
Poppy Heads, French	lb.	.40	.45
" " German	lb.	.20	.25
Potash	lb.	.06	.07
" by cask, 400 lbs.	lb.	.05½	....
" Conc., Babbitt's, balls, cases, 48 lbs.	case.	3.50	....
" " " " 24 lbs.	case.	1.75	....
" " " cans, " 48 lbs.	case.	3.50	....
" " " " " 24 lbs.	case.	1.75	....
Potassa, Caustic, Common, 1 lb. bots	lb.	.55	.60
" " White, 1 lb. "	lb.	.60	.65
" Solution (Liquor Potassæ)	lb.	.17	.20
Potassium, Acetate, 1 lb. bots	lb.	.34	.38
" Bicarbonate, 1 lb. bots	lb.	.24	.25
" Bichromate	lb.	.18	.20
" Bromide, 1 lb. bots	lb.	.50	.55
" Chlorate, English	lb.	.20	.25
" " " Powdered	lb.	.25	.30
" " French	lb.	.28	.30
" " " Powdered	lb.	.35	.40
" Chromate, pure	lb.	1.50	1.60
" " Yellow	lb.	.50	.55
" Citrate, 1 lb. bots	lb.	.68	.70
" Cyanide, Fused	lb.	.50	.55
" " Granular	lb.	.80	.83
" " Purified	lb.	.95	1.00
" Iodide, 1 lb. bots	lb.	4.65	4.75
" Permanganate, Crystals, 1 lb. bots.	lb.	.80	.85
" " " 1 oz. "	oz.	.09	.12

Potassium, Permanganate, Ord. (Cham. Min.),

	1 lb. bots.....................lb.	$	.60	$	.65

"	Prussiate, Red ....lb.	.75	.80
"	" Yellow...............lb.	.30	.32
"	Sulphate, Crystals ....lb.	.12	.15
"	" Powdered ....lb.	.15	.18
"	Sulphuret.....................lb.	.25	.32
Powder, Aromatic, 1 lb. bots...........lb.		1.50	1.75
"	Composition, bulk................lb.	.25	.30
"	" 4 oz. papers ....lb.	.35	.40
"	" 2 oz. " ....lb.	.40	.45
"	" 1 oz. " ....lb.	.45	.50
"	Dover's U. S. P.................lb.	1.30	1.40
"	Insect, true Dalmatian.............lb.	.65	.70
"	" " Roland's, in bots. (see page 70).		
Quassia Chips....................... ......lb.		.07	.10
"	Powdered.......................lb.	.18	.20
Quinia, Bromide, 1 oz....................oz.		4.50	....
"	Sulphate, French, 1 oz. bots.. ...oz.	3.30	....
"	" Hospital, 1 oz. " ......cz.	2.35	...
"	" P. & W., ⅛ oz. " ......oz.	3.75	....
"	" P. & W., 1 oz. " ......oz.	3.35	....
"	" P. & W., 5 and 10 oz. cans.oz.	3.30	...
"	Valerianate, ⅛ oz. oz.	5.50	....
Quinidia, Pure, 1 oz. bots ....oz.		2.25	2.35
"	Sulphate, 1 oz " ....oz.	1.75	1.85
Resin, White...............................lb.		.06	.08
"	" by bbl..... ....bbl.	4.50	6.00
"	Yellow ....lb.	.03	.04
"	" by bbl.... ....bbl.	2.25	2.50
"	" Powdered. ... .lb.	.20	.25
Root, Aconite, English ....lb.		.65	.70
"	" German ....lb.	.15	.18
"	" " Powdered ... .lb.	.25	.30
"	Althea (Marsh-Mallow)...........lb.	.20	.25
"	" Cut ....lb.	.22	.27
"	" Powdered........... ....lb.	.30	.35
"	Alkanet.........................lb.	.14	.18
"	" Powdered ....lb.	.25	.28
"	Blood ....lb.	.12	.15
"	" Powdered.....................lb.	.20	.25
"	Burdock ....lb.	.18	.20
"	Calamus, Peeled... ....lb.	.15	.18
"	" White, Peeled and Split......lb.	.35	.38
"	" Powdered.................lb.	.30	.35
"	Cohosh, Black....................lb.	.12	.15
"	Colchicum, English..............lb.	.40	.45
"	" German ....lb.	.15	.18
"	" " Powdered........lb.	.25	.30
"	Colombo.........................lb.	.15	.18
"	" Ground ....lb.	.18	.20
"	" Powdered ....lb.	.20	.25
"	Coltsfoot.... ....lb.	.50	.60
"	Comfrey ....lb.	.18	.20
"	" Ground...................lb.	.22	.25
"	Culver's (Black Root). ....lb.	.18	.20
"	" Powdered..............lb.	.25	.30
"	Curcuma.........................lb.	.10	.12
"	" Ground ....lb.	.12	.15
"	Dandelion ....lb.	.12	.15
"	" Cut ....lb.	.15	.20
"	" Powdered ... .lb.	.25	.30
"	Elecampane.....................lb.	.10	.12
"	" Ground ....lb.	.12	.15
"	" Powdered ....lb.	.20	.25
"	Galangal.......................lb.	.12	.15
"	" Powdered................lb.	.25	.30
"	Gentian.........................lb.	.08	.10
"	" Cut ....lb.	.10	.12
"	" Ground... ....lb.	.10	.12
"	" Powdered................lb.	.15	.18
"	Ginger, African..... .... lb.	.08	.10
"	" " Powdered............lb.	.12	.15
"	" " in cans, S. R. V. D. & Co's (see page 61).		
"	" Jamaica, Bleached............lb.	.24	.26
"	" " " Ground......lb.	.27	.30

					$	$
Root, Ginger, Jamaica, Unbleached				lb.	.22	.24
"	Ginseng			lb.	1.25	1.35
"	"	Powdered		lb.	1.40	1.50
"	Golden Seal			lb.	.15	.18
"	"	" Powdered		lb.	.22	.25
"	Hellebore, Black			lb.	.18	.20
"	"	" Powdered		lb.	.25	.28
"	"	White		lb.	.15	.18
"	"	" Powdered		lb.	.18	.20
"	Indian Hemp, Black			lb.	.25	.30
"	"	" White		lb.	.25	.30
"	Ipecac, Rio			lb.	1.45	1.50
"	"	" Powdered		lb.	1.60	1.70
"	Jalap			lb.	.30	.35
"	"	Powdered		lb.	.40	.45
"	Licorice, bundles, 10 lbs., Extra			lb.	.12	.15
"	"	" 10 lbs., No. 1		lb.	.10	.12
"	"	Ground		lb.	.12	.15
"	"	Powdered		lb.	.12	.15
"	Mandrake			lb.	.10	.12
"	"	Powdered		lb.	.18	.20
"	Orris, Finger			lb.	.50	.60
"	"	Florentine		lb.	.22	.25
"	"	" Powdered		lb.	.30	.35
"	"	Verona		lb.	.15	.18
"	"	Powdered		lb.	.20	.25
"	Pink (Spigelia)			lb.	.50	.55
"	"	Powdered		lb.	.60	.65
"	Rhatany			lb.	.22	.25
"	"	Powdered		lb.	.30	.35
"	Rhubarb, East India			lb.	.75	.90
"	"	" " Powdered		lb.	.90	1.00
"	"	" " Extra		lb.	1.25	1.50
"	"	" " " Powdered		lb.	1.50	1.75
"	"	" " Cut, extra		lb.	2.50	3.00
"	"	" " " No. 1		lb.	2.00	2.50
"	"	" " " 2		lb.	1.50	2.00
"	Sanguinaria, (Blood Root)			lb.	.10	.12
"	"	Powdered		lb.	.18	.20
"	Sarsaparilla, Honduras			lb.	.35	.40
"	"	" Cut		lb.	.40	.45
"	"	" Ground		lb.	.42	.47
"	"	" Powdered		lb.	.45	.50
"	Seneca			lb.	.75	.85
"	"	Powdered		lb.	.90	.95
"	Snake, Canada, select			lb.	.30	.35
"	"	Virginia		lb.	.35	.40
"	"	" Powdered		lb.	.45	.50
"	Squill, White			lb.	.12	.15
"	"	" Powdered, 1 lb. bots		lb.	.40	.45
"	Valerian, English			lb.	.25	.30
"	"	" Powdered		lb.	.35	.40
"	Veratrum Viride			lb.	.25	.30
"	"	" Powdered		lb.	.35	.40
"	Yellow Dock			lb.	.12	.15
"	"	" Ground		lb.	.15	.18
"	"	" Powdered		lb.	.25	.30
Rose Pink, English				lb.	.12	.15
Sago, Flour				lb.	.10	.12
" Pearl				lb.	.08	.10
Sal Acetosella				lb.	.28	.30
" Epsom				lb.	.03	.04
" " by bbl				lb.	.01¾	....
" Glauber				lb.	.03	.04
" " by bbl				lb.	.01¼	....
" Nitre, crude				lb.	.06	.07
" " Refined, commercial				lb.	.07	.08
" " " " by keg, 100 lbs.				lb.	.06	...
" " " Pure				lb.	.10	.12
" " " " by keg, 100 lbs				lb.	.09	....
" " " Double				lb.	.12	.14
" " " " by keg, 100 lbs				lb.	.10	....
" " " Triple				lb.	.13	.15
" " " " by keg, 100 lbs				lb.	.10½	....
" " " Pure, Granular				lb.	.12	.14
" " " " Powdered				lb.	.12	.15

Sal Prunel	lb.	$ .40	$ .45
" Rochelle	lb.	.34	.36
" Soda	lb.	.02	.03
" " by cask, 400 lbs.	lb.	.01⅝	....
" " by keg, 112 lbs	lb.	.01¾	....
" Tartar (Potassium Carbonate)	lb.	.14	.16
Saleratus, Pearlash	lb.	.12	.15
" in papers, S. R. V. D. & Co's (see page 69).			
Salicin, 1 oz. bots	oz.	.40	.45
Sand, White	bbl.	1.25	....
Santonin, 1 oz. bots	oz.	.70	.75
Seed, Anise	lb.	.16	.18
" " Powdered	lb.	.22	.25
" " Star	lb.	.40	.45
" Canary, Sicily	lb.	.05	.06
" " Smyrna	lb.	.04	.05
" " " by bag	bush.	2.00	....
" Caraway	lb.	.10	.12
" " Powdered	lb.	.20	.25
" Cardamom, Aleppo	lb.	2.50	2.75
" " Malabar	lb.	2.75	3.00
" " " Powdered	lb.	2.75	3.00
" " White, Extra Large	lb.	3.00	3.25
" Celery	lb.	.18	.20
" " Ground	lb.	.25	.28
" Colchicum, English	lb.	.65	.75
" " German	lb.	.22	.25
" " " Powdered	lb.	.35	.40
" Coriander	lb.	.10	.12
" " Powdered	lb.	.18	.20
" Cumin	lb.	.18	.20
" " Powdered	lb.	.25	.30
" Fennel	lb.	.18	.20
" " Powdered	lb.	.25	.30
" Flax, Clean	lb.	.05	.06
" " " by bbl	bbl.	8.00	....
" " Ground	lb.	.06	.08
" " Ground, by bbl.	lb.	.05	....
" Fœnugreek	lb.	.06	.08
" " Powdered	lb.	.09	.10
" Hemp, Russian	lb.	.05	.06
" " " by bag	bush.	1.40	....
" Larkspur	lb.	1.60	1.75
" Lobelia	lb.	.30	.35
" " Powdered	lb.	.38	.40
" Maw (Poppy)	lb.	.15	.18
" Millet	lb.	.08	.10
" Mustard, Brown, Trieste	lb.	.08	.10
" " " Ground	lb.	.18	.22
" " " Yellow	lb.	.08	.10
" Quince	lb.	.75	.85
" Rape, English	lb.	.07	.08
" " " by bag	bush.	3.00	....
" Worm, Foreign (Levant)	lb.	.18	.20
" " " Powdered	lb.	.25	.30
Seidlitz Mixture	lb.	.30	.35
" Powders, full weight and extra weight, S. R. V. D. & Co's (see page 66).			
Silver Leaf, in packs 20 books	pack.	2.00	2.25
" Nitrate, Crystals, pure	oz.	.81	.84
Snuff, Maccaboy, Lorillard's, in 4, 8, 15 and 20 lb. jars	lb.	.62	....
" Rappee, Lorillard's, in 4, 8, 15 & 20 lb. jars	lb.	.62	....
" Scotch, " in bladders	lb.	.50	....
Soap, Castile, Mottled, by box, 35 lbs. or less	lb.	.08	.10
" " Pure, by box, 35 lbs, "	lb.	.11	.12
" " " " in cks., by bx. 50 lbs	lb.	.14	....
" " White, "Conti's," by bx. 35 lb. or less	lb.	.14	.16
" " " " in cakes, by box 45 lbs	lb.	.16	....
" " " Powdered	lb.	.45	.50
" Whale Oil	lb.	.08	.10
" " " 1 lb. cans	doz.	2.00	....
Soda, Ash	lb.	.05	.06
" " by bbl	lb.	.02¾	....
" Acetate, 1 lb. bots	lb.	.40	.45
" Bi-Carbonate, American	lb.	.05	.06

Soda, Bi-Carbonate, American, by keg, 112 lbs.	lb. $	.04	....
" " English, by keg, 112 lbs.	lb.	.04¼	....
" " in pap's, S. R. V. D. & Co's (see page 69).			
" " Chem. Pure, 1 lb. bots...	lb.	.40 $	.45
" Caustic, by drum, 600 lbs...	lb.	.04½	....
" " by jar, 10 to 30 lbs....	lb.	.10	.12
" Chlorinated Solution, G. S. bots.....	doz.	2.75	3.00
" " " C. S. "	doz.	2.25	2.50
" Nitrate, crude........................	lb.	.06	.07
" " Purified.................	lb.	.16	.18
" Powders......	doz.	1.50	....
Sodium, Bromide, 1 lb. bots.................	lb.	.52	.55
" " 1 oz. "	oz.	.06	.08
" Carbonate, Chem. pure Crys., 1 lb. bots.	lb.	.40	.45
" Hypophosphite, 1 lb. bots...........	lb.	2.50	2.60
" " 1 oz. "	oz.	.18	.20
" Hyposulphite....................	lb.	.05	.08
" " in kegs.............	lb.	.04	...
" " Chem. Pure..........	lb.	.70	.80
" Phosphate, 1 lb. bots.............	lb.	.21	.22
" Salicylate, 1 oz. bots.............	oz.	.24	.27
" Silicate, Dry....................	lb.	.10	.15
" " Solution	gall.	.50	.60
" Sulphite, Crystals, 1 lb. bots	lb.	.22	.25
" " Granular, 1 lb. "	lb.	.41	.44
Spermaceti, in cakes................	lb.	.30	.35
" " by box, 40 lbs..........	lb.	.30	...
Spirits Ammonia, 1 lb. bots.................	lb.	.43	.45
" " Aromatic, 1 lb. bots........	lb.	.48	.50
" Camphor, 1 lb. bots	lb.	.50	.55
" Juniper, Comp., 1 lb. bots...........	lb.	.50	.55
" Lavender, 1 lb. "	lb.	.43	.45
" " Comp., 1 lb. "	lb.	.45	.50
" Mindererus, 1 lb. bots	lb.	.25	30
" Niter, U. S. P.....................	lb.	.38	.43
" Niter, FFFF..................	lb.	.33	.38
" " FFF	lb.	.28	.33
" Turpentine	gall.	.51	.53
" " by bbl..............	gall.	.49	....
" " in small bottles (see page 35).			
Starch, Highland, " Best," 6 pack. 38 to 42 lb. bxs.		.05	
" " " Enamel," 6 lb. slide cover			
boxes, 72 lb. crates......		.07½	...
" Duryea's, sup. 6 pack. 38 to 42 lb. boxes...		.06½	...
" " 1 lb. pack. 40 lb. boxes...		.07	...
" " Satin Gloss, 5 lb. p. b. 30 lb. boxes		.08½	...
" " " 1 lb. pack. 40 lb. boxes..		.08½	...
" " " 6 lb. s. c. bxs. 72 lb. crts.		.09	....
" " Pearl, 6 lb. pck, 38 to 42 lb. boxes.		.06	....
" Kingsford, Pure, 6 lb. pack. 38 to 45 lb. " ..		.07	....
" " 1 lb. pack. 36 lb. " ..		.07	....
" " Silver Gloss, 4 lb. p. b. 40 lb." ..		.08½	...
" " " 1 lb. pack. 36 lb. " ..		.08½	...
" " " 6 lb. s. c. b, 72 lb. crts.		.09	....
" " Pearl, 6 bund. 38 to 45 lb. boxes.		.06	....
" Duryea's Improv. Corn, 1 lb. pck. 40 lb. bxs		.09	....
" " " ½ lb. pck. 40 lb. " .		.09½	....
" Kingsford's Oswego Corn, 1 lb. pk. 40 lb. " .		.09	....
" " " 1 lb. pk. 20 lb. " .		.09	...
Discount 5 per cent.			
Stone, Pumice............................	lb.	.04	.06
" " Select	lb.	.05	.07
" " Powdered...................	lb.	.04	.06
" Rotten, English.....................	lb.	.08	.10
" : " Powdered............	lb.	.06	.08
" Soap, Powdered	lb.	.05	.07
Strontium, Nitrate......................	lb.	.19	.20
Strychnia, Crystals, ⅛ oz. bots...........	oz.	1.75	1.80
" " Powdered, ⅛ oz. "	oz.	1.60	1.65
" " Sulphate, ⅛ oz. "	oz.	1.60	1.65
Styrax, Liquid.......................	lb.	.30	.35
Sugar of Milk, Crystals	lb.	.40	.45
" " Granular........	lb.	.45	.50
" " Powdered..........	lb.	.45	.50
Sulphur Flowers......................	lb.	.04	.05
" " by bbl., 175 lbs.............	lb.	.03¼	....

Sulphur Lac ....lb.	$	.12	$	.15
" Rolls (Brimstone)................lb.		.03		.04
" " by bbl......................lb.		.02½		....
Syrups, Officinal (see page 28).				
Tamarinds ....lb.		.09		.11
Tapioca, E. I.......................lb.		.08		.10
" Pearl...........................lb.		.10		.12
Tar, Barbadoes.....................gall.		.90		1.00
" Common, by bbl..................bbl.		2.75		....
" Pure N. C., 5 gall. cans, 2 cans in case..gall.		.20		....
" " " 1 " " 1 doz." " ..doz.		4.00		....
" " " ½ " " 2 " " " ..doz.		2.25		....
" " " · 1 quart " 2 " " " ..doz.		1.50		....
" " " 1 pint " 4 " " " ..doz.		.85		....
" " " ½ " " 6 " " " ..doz.		.75		....
Tartar Emetic, Crystals.................lb.		.81		.83
" " Powdered (Antimony Tart.)...lb.		.71		.73
Tin Foil, Medium ....lb.		.25		.30
" " Tissue ....lb.		.30		.35
" " Tobacco.....................lb.		.25		.30
" Muriate, Crystals..................lb.		.23		.25
" " Solution (Madder Compound)..lb.		.12		.15
Tinctures, Officinal (see pages 27 and 28).				
Tow, Surgeons'.......................lb.		.25		.30
Turpentine, Venice, true, 1 lb. bot.........bot.		.30		.35
" White......................lb.		.08		.10
Vaccine Virus, Quill Slips ....each.		.25		....
" " Capillary Tubes...........each.		1.00		....
" " Crusts ....each.		2.00		....
Veratria, Pure. ½ oz. bots..............oz.		2.20		2.25
Verdigris, in balls....................lb.		.38		.40
" Distilled.....................lb.		.70		.75
" Powdered ....lb.		.50		.55
Vinegar of Squill....................lb.		.40		.50
Water, Cologne, "Perfection"...........gall.		6.00		6.50
" " " in toilet bottles (see page 65).				
" Distilled ....gall.		.20		.25
" Javelle.......................gall.		.75		....
" " in bots..................doz.		4.00		4.50
" Lime ....gall.		.50		....
" Orange Flower, Trip. Fr. Chiris'.... .gall.		2.25		2.50
" " " " " " small...doz.		1.75		2.00
" " " " " " medium.doz.		2.75		3.00
" " " " " " large ..doz.		3.50		3.75
" Rose, Triple, French, Chiris'.......gall.		2.50		2.75
" " " " " small....doz.		2.00		2.25
" " " " " medium..doz.		3.00		3.25
" " " " " large ...doz.		4.00		4.25
Wax, Bayberry.......................lb.		.25		.30
" Bees', Yellow......................lb.		.28		.30
" " " select................lb.		.33		.35
" " " select small cakes........lb.		.40		.45
" Japan. ....lb.		.22		.25
" White, Pure, Philips'.............lb.		.50		.55
" " " " by box, 50 lbs....lb.		.45		....
" " " " Star.............lb.		.55		.57
" " " " " by box, 50 lbs.......lb.		.50		....
" " small cakes...............lb.		.65		.70
Wood, Guaiac, Rasped ....lb.		.04		.06
" Sandal ....lb.		.50		.60
Zinc, Acetate, 1 lb. bots..................lb.		.58		.60
" Bromide, 1 oz. " ....oz.		.20		.25
" Carbonate, Precip., 1 lb. bots..........lb.		.28		.30
" Chloride, Fused, 1 oz. " ....oz.		.08		.10
" " Granular, 1 oz. " ....oz.		.08		.10
" " Solution, Com'l., 1 lb. bots...lb.		.11		.12
" " " Medicinal, 1 lb. bots.lb.		.22		.25
" Cyanide, 1 oz. bots...................oz.		.25		.30
" Iodide, 1 oz. bots..................oz.		.60		.65
" Oxide, true, 1 lb. bots..... ....lb.		.12		.15
" Phosphate, 1 lb. " ....lb.		2.00		2.10
" Sulphate, Crystals ....lb.		.06		.08
" Valerianate, 1 oz., ¼ oz., and ⅛ oz. bots.oz.		.33		.35

DYE-WOODS.

Bar Wood, Ground	in bbls., about	130 lbs	..lb..	$	.03
Brazil Wood, Ground	"	"	130 "	..lb.	.04
Cam Wood, Ground	"	"	130 "	..lb.	.05
Fustic, Cut,	"	"	130 "	..lb.	.02
Fustic, Ground	"	"	130 "	..lb.	.02¼
Fustic, Cuba, Cut	"	"	130 "	..lb.	.02¼
Fustic, Cuba, Ground	"	"	130 "	..lb.	.02½
Hypernic, Cut	"	"	120 "	..lb.	.04
Hypernic, Ground	"	"	120 "	..lb.	.04¼
Logwood, St. Domingo, Cut	"	"	130 "	..lb.	.02
Log Wood, St. Domingo, Gr'd	"	"	130 "	..lb.	.02¼
Log Wood, Campeachy, Cut	"	"	130 "	..lb.	.02
Log Wood, Campeachy, Gr'd	"	"	130 "	..lb.	.02¼
Nic Wood, Cut	"	"	120 "	..lb.	.03
Peach Wood, Ground	"	"	130 "	..lb.	.04
Red Sanders, Ground	"	"	120 "	..lb.	.03½
Red Wood, Cut	"	"	125 "	..lb.	.02½

PRESSED BARKS, HERBS AND ROOTS.

Prices quoted are for Herbs and Flowers in ounces. Roots and Barks in pounds. Herbs in halves, quarters, or pounds, 2 cents per pound less.

Aconite Leaves....	lb. $	.25
" Root	lb.	.25
Alder Bark, Black...	lb.	.20
Alum Root....	lb.	.30
Arbutus, Trailing....	lb.	.30
Arnica Flowers	lb.	.35
" Root	lb.	.40
Ash Bark, Prickly	lb.	.20
Avens Root	lb.	.35
Balm, Lemon	lb.	.40
" Sweet	lb.	.35
Balmony	lb.	.20
Balsam, Sweet	lb.	.35
Barberry Bark	lb.	.35
Basil, Sweet	lb.	.30
Beech Leaves	lb.	.25
Beth Root....	lb.	.30
Bitter Root	lb.	.35
Bittersweet, Bark of Root	lb.	.35
" Herb	lb.	.20
Blackberry Root	lb.	.15
Blessed Thistle.	lb.	.30
Blue Flag	lb.	.25
Boneset	lb.	.20
Borage	lb.	.35
Boxwood Bark	lb.	.15
Buckbean	lb.	.40
Bugle, Bitter	lb.	.30
" Sweet	lb.	.25
Burdock Leaves	lb.	.20
" Root	lb.	.20
Butterfly Weed	lb.	.25
Butternut Bark	lb.	.15
Canadian Fleabane	lb.	.25
Cancer Root Plant	lb.	.25
Catnip	lb.	.20
Centaury, American	lb.	.30
Checkerberry	lb.	.20
Chicory	lb.	.25
Cicuta Leaves	lb.	.30
Clover Heads, Red	lb.	.30
" " White	lb.	.35
Cohosh Root, Black	lb.	.15
" " Blue	lb.	.20
" " Red	lb.	.40
" " White	lb.	.25
Coltsfoot	lb.	.25
Comfrey Root	lb.	.20
Cotton Root Bark	lb.	.28
Cramp Bark	lb.	.25
Cranesbill	lb.	.20
Crowfoot	lb.	.30
Culver's Root	lb.	.20
Dandelion Herb	lb.	.25
Devil's Bit	lb.	.40
Dock, Yellow	lb.	.20
Dogwood Bark	lb.	.20
Elecampane	lb.	.20
Elder Bark	lb.	.20
" Flowers	lb.	.25
" Dwarf	lb.	.30
" Sweet	lb.	.30
Fern, Male	lb.	.25
" Sweet	lb.	.20
Feverfew	lb.	.60
Fireweed	lb.	.25
Fleabane	lb.	.30
Fox-Glove	lb.	.35
Garget	lb.	.25
Ginger, Wild	lb.	.40

```
Goldthread.....................................lb. $ .60
Golden-rod.........................    ...........lb.   .25
   "      Seal...................................lb.   .20
Green Hellebore................................lb.   .25
Hellebore, Black...............................lb.   .30
   "      White ................................lb.   .20
Hemlock Bark..................................lb.   .15
   "      Leaves ...............................lb.   .30
Henbane, Black...........................   .....lb.   .35
Hoarhound ....................................lb.   .20
Hollyhock Flowers.............................lb.   .50
Hyssop........................................lb.   .30
Indian Hemp, Black............................lb.   .35
   "      "      White .........................lb.   .28
   "      Tobacco ..............................lb.   .30
   "      Turnip ...............................lb.   .30
Indigo, Wild....................................lb.   .20
Jessamin, Yellow...............................lb.   .20
Ladies' Slipper.................................lb.   .25
Larkspur Herb.................................lb.   .40
Lettuce, Wild..................................lb.   .30
Life Everlasting................................lb.   .25
Life Root......................................lb.   .30
Liverwort......................................lb.   .35
Lobelia Herb ..................................lb.   .20
Lungwort......................................lb.   .35
Maiden Hair...................................lb.   .30
Marigold  Flowers..............................lb.   .45
Marjoram, Sweet..............................lb.   .35
Marsh Rosemary...............................lb.   .30
May Weed.....................................lb.   .25
Motherwort ...................................lb.   .25
Mullein Herb..................................lb.   .25
Parilla, Yellow .................................lb.   .20
Pennyroyal ...................................lb.   .20
Peppermint  ..................................lb.   .20
Pilewort ......................................lb.   .30
Pleurisy Root..................................lb.   .25
Poke     "     ..................................lb.   .15
Princess Feather ..............................lb.   .30
   "      Pine..................................lb.   .25
Queen-of-the-Meadow  Herb.....................lb.   .20
   "      "      "      Root.....................lb.   .20
Raspberry Leaves .............................lb.   .20
Rue ..........................................lb.   .40
Sage .........................................lb.   .20
Savin.........................................lb.   .25
Scullcap .....................................lb.   .30
Skunk-Cabbage Root...........................lb.   .25
Solomon's Seal................................lb.   .20
Southernwood.................................lb.   .35
Spearmint ....................................lb.   .20
Speedwell, Virginia............................lb.   .30
Spikenard.....................................lb.   .20
Stone Root....................................lb.   .25
Stramonium Leaves............................lb.   .20
   "      Root..................................lb.   .25
   "      Seed..................................lb.   .25
Sumach Bark..................................lb.   .18
Summer Savory...............................lb.   .25
Sweet Clover..................................lb.   .30
   "      Flag .................................lb.   .25
Tamarack Bark................................lb.   .15
Tansy, Double ................................lb.   .20
Thoroughwort.................................lb.   .20
Thyme .......................................lb.   .25
Unicorn Root..................................lb.   .30
Vervain ......................................lb.   .25
Wa-a-hoo Bark................................lb.   .35
Water Pepper.................................lb.   .20
Wintergreen ..................................lb.   .25
Wormwood ...................................lb.   .25
Yarrow.......................................lb.   .20
```

S. R. VAN DUZER'S

Officinal Fluid Extracts.

We offer the following line of Fluid Extracts of our own manufacture, prepared with great care under our own immediate supervision by Repercolation (the only proper method whereby the active principle of the drug is obtained). The standard of strength is that of the U. S. Pharmacopœia.

The following prices are for Extracts in pint bottles ; when ordered in one-half pints, add 20 cents per pint, and in one-quarter pints, add 50 cents per pint additional ; five-pint bottles, 10 cents per pint less, subject to a liberal *discount.*

TRADE NAMES.	BOTANICAL NAMES.	One pt. Bots. Per pt.
Arnica	*Arnica Montana*	$1.75
Balmony	*Chelone Glabra*	1.25
Belladonna Leaf	*Atropa Belladonna*	2.00
Bitter-root	*Apocynum Androsemfolium*	2.00
Bitter-sweet	*Solanum Dulcamara*	1.50
Black Alder	*Prinos Verticillatus*	1.50
Blackberry	*Rubus Villosus*	1.50
Black Cohosh	*Cimicifuga Racemosa*	2.00
Black Haw	*Viburnum Prunifolium*	1.75
Black Hellebore	*Helleborus Niger*	1.75
Bloodroot	*Sanguinaria*	1.75
Blue Flag	*Iris Versicolor*	1.75
Boneset	*Eupatorium Perfoliatum*	1.25
Boxwood	*Cornus Florida*	1.25
Buchu	*Barosma Crenata*	2.00
Buckthorn Bark	*Rhamnus Frangula*	1.50
Burdock	*Lappa Minor*	1.50
Butternut Bark	*Juglans Cinerea*	1.25
Calabar Bean	*Physostigma Venenosum*	6.00
Calendula		4.00
Cardamom	*Elettaria Cardamomum*	6.00
" Comp		3.00
Catnip	*Nepeta Cataria*	1.25
Cayenne Pepper	*Capsicum*	2.50
Chamomile	*Anthemis Nobilis*	1.75
Cherry Bark	*Prunus Virginiana*	1.75
Chestnut Leaves	*Castanea Vesca*	2.00
Cinchona, Aromatic		3.00
" Pale	*Cinchona Pallida*	3.00
" Compound		3.00
" Calisaya	*Cinchona Flava*	5.00
" Red	*Cinchona Rubra*	5.00
Coca Leaves	*Erythroxylon Coca*	6.00
Colchicum Root	*Colchicum Autumnale*	2.00
" Seed	" "	2.50
Colocynth	*Cucumis Colocynthis*	2.25
Colombo	*Cocculus Palmatus*	2.00
Coltsfoot	*Tussilago*	1.50
Conium Seed	*Conium Maculatum*	2.00
Cotton Root Bark	*Gossypium Herbaceum*	3.00
Cramp Bark	*Viburnum Opulus*	1.50
Cranesbill	*Geranium Maculatum*	1.75
Cubeb	*Piper Cubeba*	2.50
Culver's Root	*Leptandra Virginica*	2.00
Cundurango	*Pseusmagenuetus Equatorium*	3.00
Damiana		4.00
Dandelion	*Taraxacum*	2.00
" and Senna		1.75
" Compound		2.00
Dwarf Elder	*Aralia Hispida*	1.25
Elecampane	*Inula*	1.25

Ergot	*Ergota*	$4.00
Eucalyptus	*Eucalyptus Globulus*	4.00
Fern Sweet	*Comptonia*	1.25
Fire Weed	*Erechthites Hieracifolia*	1.50
Foxglove	*Digitalis Purpurea*	1.75
Garden Celandine	*Chelidonium*	1.50
Gelsemium	*Gelsemium Sempervirens*	2.50
Gentian	*Gentiana Lutea*	1.50
" Compound	" "	1.75
Golden Seal	*Hydrastis Canadensis*	2.00
Gravel Plant	*Epigœa Repens*	1.25
Grindelia Robusta		3.50
" Squarrosa		3.50
Guarana	*Paullinia Sorbilis*	7.00
Hemlock	*Pinus Canadensis*	1.25
Henbane	*Hyoscyamus Niger*	2.50
Hop	*Humulus Lupulus*	2.50
Horehound	*Marrubium Vulgare*	1.50
Hydrangea	*Hydrangea Arborescens*	1.75
Indian Hemp, Foreign	*Cannabis Indica*	2.50
" " White	*Asclepias Incarnate*	1.75
Ipecac	*Cephælis Ipecacuanha*	6.00
Jaborandi	*Pilocarpus Pinnatus*	3.50
Jalap	*Ipomœa Jalapa*	3.00
Kava Kava	*Piper Methysticum*	4.00
Lactucarium		9.00
Ladies' Slipper	*Cypripedium Pubescens*	2.25
Lettuce	*Lactuca Sativa*	1.50
Liquorice	*Glycyrrhiza Glabra*	1.50
Liverwort	*Hepatica Americana*	1.50
Lobelia	*Lobelia Inflata*	1.75
Logwood	*Hæmatoxylon Campech*	1.25
Lupulin	*Lupulina*	3.50
Male Fern	*Aspidium Filix Mas*	1.50
Mandrake	*Podophyllum Peltatum*	1.75
Matico	*Artanthe Elongata*	3.00
Nux Vomica	*Strychnos Nux Vomica*	2.25
Opium, Aqueous	*Papaver Somnifera*	3.50
Pareira Brava	*Cissampelos Pareira*	2.50
Pink Root	*Spigelia Marilandica*	2.50
" " and Senna		2.00
Pipsissewa	*Chimaphila Umbellata*	1.50
Pleurisy Root	*Asclepias Tuberosa*	2.00
Poison Oak	*Rhus Toxicodendron*	3.00
Poke Root	*Phytolacca Decandra*	1.50
Poppies	*Papaver Somniferum*	1.75
Prickly Ash Bark	*Xanthoxylum Fraxineum*	1.75
Pulsatilla	*Anemone Pulsatilla*	2.50
Quassia	*Quassia Excelsa*	1.50
Queen of the Meadow	*Eupatorium Purpureum*	1.50
Red Clover Tops	*Trifolium Pratense*	2.00
Rhatany	*Krameria Triandra*	2.00
Rhubarb	*Rheum Palmatum*	4.00
" Aromatic		4.00
" and Senna		3.00
Sarsaparilla	*Smilax Officinalis*	2.25
" Comp. U. S. P		2.25
" American	*Smilax Sarsaparilla*	1.75
Savin	*Juniperus Sabina*	1.50
Scullcap	*Scutellaria Lateriflora*	2.00
Sea Wrack	*Fucus Vesiculosus*	2.00
Seneka	*Polygala Senega*	3.50
Senna	*Cassia Acutifolia*	1.50
" Aqueous		1.50
Skunk Cabbage	*Symplocarpus Fœtidus*	1.25
Snakeroot	*Serpentaria*	2.50
Squill	*Scilla Maritima*	1.50
" Acetic	" "	1.50
" Compound	" "	3.00
Stillingia	*Stillingia Sylvatica*	2.50
" Compound		2.50
Stone Root	*Collinsonia Canadensis*	1.75
Stramonium Seed	*Datura Stramonium*	1.75
Sumach	*Rhus Glabrum*	1.25
Sundew	*Drosera Rotundifolia*	4.50
Unicorn	*Aletris Farinosa*	3.00

Unicorn False............	...*Helonias Dioica*.......	$3.00
Uva Ursi.....	...*Arctostaphylos*	1.50
Valerian.....	*Valeriana Officinalis*.......	2.00
Water Pepper...........	*Polygonum Punctatum*....	1.25
Wild Indigo	*Baptisia Tinctoria*.........	1.50
Wild Turnip...........	*Arum Triphyllum*	1.50
Wild Yam......	*Dioscorea Villosa*..........	1.25
Witch Hazel...........	*Hamamelis Virginica*......	1.25
Wormwood........	*Artemisia Absinthium*.....	1.25
Yellow Dock	*Rumex Cripus*.............	2.00
Yerba Santa............	*Eriodictyon Californicum*...	4.00

EXTRACTS, SOLID—S. R. Van Duzer's.

Aconite Leaves................	lb.	2.00
" Root	lb.	3.00
Aloes, Soc....................................	lb.	2.00
Belladonna Leaf............................: ...	lb.	3.00
" Root	lb.	4.00
Butternut	lb.	1.25
Cannabis Indicus..	oz.	.50
Chamomile................................	lb.	1.75
Colchicum Root, acetic..........	lb.	4.00
" " " English	oz.	.50
Colocynth, Comp., U. S. P..................	lb.	4.00
" " " Powdered........... .	lb.	4.50
" Simple	lb.	3.00
Conium....	lb.	1.75
Cotton Root Bark.....	lb.	3.75
Dandelion 85	lb.	.85
Digitalis	lb.	2.25
Ergot	oz.	.50
Gentian, U. S. P...	lb.	.75
Guarana......	oz.	1.00
Guaiac Wood........	oz.	.40
Hellebore, Black.............................	lb.	2.50
Hop	lb.	3.00
Hyoscyamus	lb.	3.00
Ignatia Beans.....	oz.	1.00
Ipecac....................................	oz.	1.00
Jaborandi................................	oz.	.75
Jalap	lb.	3.00
Lettuce.......................................	lb.	2.25
Licorice	lb.	1.00
Lupulin....................................	lb.	3.50
Mandrake..................................	lb.	2.50
Nux Vomica............................. ...	lb.	4.00
Opium	oz.	1.00
" dried..................................	oz.	1.50
Quassia...	lb.	2.75
Rhatany	lb.	3.00
Rhubarb...................................	lb.	4.50
Sarsaparilla, Comp.........................	lb.	2.75
" Simple	lb.	3.50
Sea Wrack.................................	oz.	.25
Senna	lb.	2.00
Serpentaria	oz.	.50
Stramonium Leaf...........................	lb.	2.50
Sumbul.....	oz.	1.50
Valerian	lb.	3.25
Verat. Viride................................	lb.	3.25

GELATINE & SUGAR COATED PILLS AND GRANULES

Of the U. S. Pharmacopœia and other reliable Formulas.

We carry in stock a full line of Messrs. Reed & Carnrick's (Gelatine and Sugar Coated) Pills, Elixirs, and their other standard preparations, believing them to be most reliable, and send them in all cases, unless special makes are specified. Prices subject to the usual liberal discount.

TINCTURES—S. R. Van Duzer's.

Made after Officinal and other Formulas.

Tincture	Aconite Leaf	lb. $	.50
"	" Root	lb.	.75
"	" " Fleming's	lb.	.90
"	Alkanet	lb.	.50
"	Aloes	lb.	.50
"	" Comp	lb.	.75
"	Ambergris	lb.	4.00
"	Arnica	lb.	.50
"	Assafœtida	lb.	.60
"	Belladonna	lb.	.50
"	Benzoin	lb.	.75
"	" Comp.	lb.	.75
"	Blood Root	lb.	.50
"	Buchu	lb.	.50
"	Calabar Bean	lb.	.90
"	Cannabis Indica	lb.	.90
"	Cantharides	lb.	.70
"	Capsicum	lb.	.50
"	Cardamom	lb.	.75
"	" Comp	lb.	.60
"	Cascarilla	lb.	.50
"	Castor	lb.	.90
"	Catechu	lb.	.60
"	Cherry Bark	lb.	.60
"	Cimicifuga	lb.	.60
"	Cinchona	lb.	.60
"	" Comp	lb.	.60
"	Cocculus Indicus	lb.	.60
"	Cochineal	lb.	.60
"	Colchicum Root	lb.	.60
"	" Seed	lb.	.60
"	Colocynth	lb.	.60
"	Colombo	lb.	.50
"	Conium	lb.	.50
"	Cubeb	lb.	.50
"	Curcuma	lb.	.50
"	Ergot	lb.	.60
"	" Ethereal	lb.	.75
"	Galls	lb.	.50
"	Gentian, Comp	lb.	.50
"	Ginger	lb.	.60
"	Guaiac	lb.	.70
"	" Ammoniated	lb.	.85
"	Guarana	lb.	1.50
"	Hellebore	lb.	.50
"	Hop	lb.	.60
"	Hyoscyamus	lb.	.50
"	Iodine	lb.	1.00
"	" Colorless	lb.	1.25
"	" Comp	lb.	1.25
"	Ipecac	lb.	.75
"	Iron, Acet	lb.	.50
"	" Muriate	lb.	.35
"	" " Tasteless	lb.	.75
"	Jalap	lb.	.75
"	Kino	lb.	.60
"	Larkspur	lb.	.80
"	Lobelia	lb.	.50
"	" Ethereal	lb.	.60
"	" and Capsicum	lb.	.70
"	Lupulin	lb.	.90
"	Matico	lb.	.75
"	Musk	lb.	1.50
"	Myrrh	lb.	.65
"	Nux Vomica	lb.	.65
"	Opium, U. S. P	lb.	1.00
"	" Camph	lb.	.50
"	" Deodorized	lb.	1.75
"	Orange Peel, Bitter	lb.	.50
"	" " Sweet	lb.	.50
"	Orris	lb.	.50

Tincture, Pimpinella	lb. $	.50
" Poke Root	lb.	.50
" Prickly Ash	lb.	.50
" Pulsatilla	lb.	.50
" Quassia	lb.	.50
" Rhatany	lb.	.50
" Red Saunders	lb.	.50
" Rhubarb	lb.	.60
" " Aqueous	lb.	.50
" " Aromatic	lb.	.70
" " and Aloes	lb.	.60
" Saffron Am	lb.	.60
" " Spanish	lb.	1.50
" Scullcap	lb.	.60
" Senega	lb.	.60
" Senna	lb.	.50
" " Comp	lb.	.50
" Serpentaria	lb.	.50
" Soap, Camphorated	lb.	.50
" Squill	lb.	.50
" Stramonium	lb.	.50
" " Leaf	lb.	.50
" " Seed	lb.	.50
" Styrax	lb.	.60
" Tolu	lb.	.70
" Valerian	lb.	.50
" " Ammoniated	lb.	.80
" Veratrum Viride	lb.	.75
" Warburg's, 1 lb. bots	lb.	4.50
" " 1 oz. "	doz.	4.50

SYRUPS—S. R. Van Duzer's.

Made after Officinal and other Formulas.

Syrup, Banana, for Soda-Water	gall.	2.00
" Blackberry, " "	gall.	2.00
" Garlic	lb.	.60
" Ginger, for Soda-Water	gall.	2.00
" Iodide Iron, 1 lb. bots	lb.	.65
" " " and Manganese, 1 lb. bots	lb.	.90
" " Manganese, 1 lb. bots	lb.	.90
" Ipecac	lb.	.60
" Lactucarium	lb.	1.00
" Lemon, for Soda-Water	gall.	2.00
" Lime	lb.	.50
" Orange Peel	lb.	.50
" Pine-apple, for Soda-Water	gall.	2.00
" Poppy, 1 lb. bots	lb.	.50
" Protoxide Iron, 1 lb. bots	lb.	.70
" Pyrophosphate Iron, 1 lb. bots	lb.	.70
" Raspberry, for Soda-Water	gall.	2.00
" Rhubarb	lb.	.60
" " Aromatic	lb.	.50
" " and Potass	lb.	.65
" Sarsaparilla	lb.	.50
" " Comp	lb.	.50
" " for Soda Water	gall.	2.50
" Senna	lb.	.50
" Senega	lb.	.60
" Simple	lb.	.15
" Squill	lb.	.50
" " Comp. (Cox's Hive)	lb.	.50
" Stillingia	lb.	.60
" " Comp	lb.	.60
" Strawberry, for Soda-Water	gall.	2.00
" Tar	lb.	.50
" Tolu	lb.	.60
" Vanilla, for Soda-Water	gall.	3.00
" Wild Cherry	lb.	.50

SPIRITS—S. R. Van Duzer's.

Made after Officinal and other Formulas.

Spirits Ammonia, 1 lb. bots........ .... lb. $ .45
  "   "   Aromatic, 1 lb. bots............ ....lb.   .50
  "   Camphor, 1 lb. bots........................lb.   .50
  "   Chloroform, U. S. P., 1 lb. bots............lb.   .80
  "   Juniper, 1 lb. bots.........................lb.   .50
  "   "   Comp, 1 lb. bots..................lb.   .50
  "   Lavender,   1 lb. " ....lb.   .50
  "   "   Comp., 1 lb. " ....lb.   .45
  "   Horse-radish, 1 lb. " ... .lb.   .75
  "   Melissa,   1 lb. " ....lb.   1.00 .
  "   Mindererus (Liq. Ammon., Acet.), 1 lb. bots.lb.   .25
  "   Nutmeg,   1 lb. bots......... ....lb.   .45
  "   Pimento, 1 lb. " ....lb.   .45
  "   Rosemary, 1 lb. " ....lb.   .45

WINES—S. R. Van Duzer's.

Made after Officinal and other Formulas.

Wine Aloes.............................. ....lb.   .60
  "   Antimony ....lb.   .75
  "   Aromatic ....lb.   .75
  "   Colchicum Root....................... ...lb.   .75
  "   "   Seed ....lb.   .75
  "   Ergot .... lb.   .90
  "   Ipecac ....lb.   .90
  "   Iron........................... ..lb.   .70
  "   Opium .... lb.   2.00
  "   Rhubarb .. ..lb.   .90
  "   Tar ....lb.   .70
  "   Tobacco ....lb.   .75

CORKS.

TAPERED CORKS.

	XX	X			XX	X
	Per Gross.				Per Gross.	
Assorted 1 to 6...	$0.45	$0.12	No.	12.....	$1.80	.94
" 3 to 6...	.50	.16		13.....	2.00	1.05
No. 00 and 0.....	.28	.07		14....	2.25	1.25
1.....	.30	.08		15...	2.50	1.38
2.....	.33	.10		16..	2.75	1.52
3.....	.38	.12		17....	3.00	1.80
4.....	.47	.14		18....	3.25	1.94
5.....	.56	.17		19....	3.50	2.10
6.....	.67	.22		20....	3.75	2.25
7.....	.83	.35		22....	4.50	2.70
8.....	1.00	.47		24...	5.50	3.00
9.....	1.20	.55		26...	6.50	3.30
10.....	1.40	.66	Assorted 6 to 10..	1.10	.46	
11.....	1.60	.80	" 11 to 20..	2.75	1.50	

EXTRA LONG TAPERED CORKS.

	XX	X			XX	X
	Per Gross.				Per Gross.	
No. 0.........	$0.34	$0.08	No. 6.........	$0.90	$0.25	
1.........	.36	.09	7.........	1.05	.39	
2.........	.42	.11	8.........	1.25	.55	
3.........	.50	.13	9.........	1.55	.66	
4.........	.60	.16	10.........	1.92	.79	
5.........	.72	.20				

STRAIGHT WINE CORKS.

		XX	X
		1½ in. long.	1¼ in. long.
No. 6....................	per gross,	$1.10	$0.44
7.....................	"	1.25	.55
8.....................	"	1.45	.67
9.....................	"	1.60	.73
10.....................	"	1.75	.79

COMMON TAPERED FLASK, BOTTLE AND DEMIJOHN CORKS.

		Per Gross.
No. 1,	}	
2,	Suitable for Inks and Bluing..........	$0.03
3,		.04
4,		.05
		.06
5,	Suitable for ½ pint Flasks...............	.09
6,		.12
7,	" " 1 " "	.16
8,		.23
9,	" " quarts "	.30
10,		.38
11,..	" " ½ gallon Demijohns..........	.45
12,..	" " 1 gallon "	.50
13,	" " 2 " "	.54
14,		.58
15,	" " 3 " "	.63
16,		.68
17,	" " 5 " "	.74
18,		.80
19,		.87
20,		.95
22,	" " Jugs and Cans....	1.15
24,		1.40
26,		1.70

Ass'd 6 to 10, for ½ pt., pint and quart bottles......... .25
Ass'd 11 to 20, for Jugs and ½ to 5 gal. Demijohns...... .70

SPECIE OR JAR CORKS.
Measure on Top or Large End.

Diameter.	Per Gr.	Diameter.	Per Gr.
1 inch..................	$0.29	2¼ inch...............	$1.43
1¼ "	.44	2½ "	1.77
1½ "	.63	2¾ "	2.23
1¾ "	.86	3 "	2.68
2 "	1.14		

		Per 100.				Per 100.
Rubber, No. 1	......$6.00		Rubber, No. 4½	......$1.50		
" " 2	.... 4.00		" " 5	...... 1.00		
" " 2½	...... 3.25		" " 6	...... .75		
" " 3	...... 2.50		" " 6½	...... .75		
" " 4	...... 1.50		" " 7	...... .75		

Wines and Liquors.

BRANDIES.

OTARD, DUPUY & CO.

Brandies, Vintage	1878.	....	per gall.	$6.00
"	"	1875	"	6.50
"	"	1872...	"	7.00
"	"	1869	"	7.50
"	"	1867	"	8.00
"	"	Royal	"	10.00
"	"	Very Old	"	12.00

WHISKIES.

Whisky, Scotch	per gall.	$5.50
"	Irish	"	5.50
"	Bourbon, very old	"	5.00
"	" Old	"	3.00
"	" New	"	2.50
"	" Rye	"	3.50

GINS.

Gins, Holland	per gall.	$3.75
"	Old Tom	"	4.00

RUM.

Rum, Jamaica	per gall.	$5.50
"	Santa Cruz	"	5.00
"	New England	"	1.75

WINES.

M. LASSALETTA & CO.

Wines, Sherry, Pale Brown ...... from $2.00 to $5.00 per gall.

SANDEMAN'S SONS & CO.

Wines, Port .... from $2.00 to $5.00 per gall.
Quality unsurpassed.

Wines, Malaga, Sweet (old) .... per gall.	$3.00
Wines, Madeira, very fine .... per gall.	$4.00

ALES.

Ale, Younger's Scotch, Casks, 8 doz. pints .... doz.	$1.90
" Bass' English,	"	8 "	" .. .. "	1.95
" " "	"	8 "	quarts ...... "	3.20

PORTER.

Porter, Guinness' (Stout) ...... Cases, 6 doz. pts. .doz.	$1.90
" " " ...... "	4 "	qts.. "	3.00
" Barclay & Perkin's Stout, Casks, 8 "	pts.. "	1.90
" " " " "	8 "	qts.. "	3.00

SPONGES.

Carriage.

			Average number sponges to the pound or string.
Florida, Sheeps' Wool, extra, select medium....... .lb.	$2.50..	5 to 8
small.................... "	1.20..	16 to 20
large.................. . "	2.50..	1 to 3
assorted sizes............... "	2.25..	6 to 10
Nassau, Sheeps' Wool, extra, select medium......... "	2.25..	5 to 8
assorted sizes.... .... "	1.75..	6 to 10
Florida, Carriage....................... "	1.00..	8 to 10
Honeycomb, Carriage............. "	.75..	10 to 12
Bahama, Carriage................... "	1.25..	10 to 12

School.

Reef, No. 1, selected.....................lb.	$1.50..	60 to 80
" No. 1, medium...................."	2.00..	40 to 60
" Slate or Yellow.................... "	1.25..	80 to 90
Hard Head, small..... .... "	1.25..100 to 125

Surgeons.

Surgeons, small.....................lb.	$2.00..	50 to 60
" medium..................... "	2.50..	25 to 30
" large..................... "	3.50..	12 to 15
" extra, select, assorted.................per box	2.50..
" on strings, small .... string	2.00..	45
No. 1................. "	4.50..	40
No. 2.................... "	1.50..	40

Bath.

Bath, Medium, Small, Large.

" Coupe, No. 1........................lb.	$2.00..	4 to 6
" " No. 2.................................. "	..	4 to 6
" Formes, No. 1....... .... "	..	8 to 10
" " No. 2.................................. "	..	10 to 12
" Best Selected (Surchoix) .... "	..	6 to 8
" Formes, No. 1, assorted ....string	10.00..	15
" " medium....... .... "	7.50..	20
" " small........................ "	2.50..	25
" " No. 2, medium.............. "	6.00..	20
" " No. 3. " ......:............. "	4.00..	20
" Best selected Surchoix, assorted on strings	13.00..	15
" " " medium on strings.........	10.00..	20

Toilet.

Fine Turkey Formes, large.....................lb.	$5.50..	10 to 12
" " medium..................... "	4.50..	14 to 16
" flat pieces or Potters'................. "	4.50..	14 to 16
" medium. cup, for Nursery......each $ .30 to 1.00..
" cup, for Toilet ....each 1.00 to 4.00..

Manufacturers.

Potters, Hatters, and Shoemakers.

Zimocca, No. 1.................................string	$4.00..	70 to 80
" No. 2........ .... "	3.00..	70 to 80
" Formes, No. 1......................lb.	3.50..	25 to 30
" " No. 2 .... "	1.75..	25 to 30
" Loose, small.......................... "	1.50..	20 to 25
" Potters', loose.....................lb. $3.00 to	4.00..	14 to 16

Cups.

Fine Turkey.
Assorted sizes, on strings, 30 to 40 pieces.......$6.00 to $20.00

CHAMOIS.

	per kip.	per dozen.			per kip.	per dozen.
X. P....kip, 30 skins,	$21.00	$8.50	F.......kip, 30 skins,	$6.00	$3 00
P...... " "	18 00	8 00	G....... " "	5.00	2.50
No. 1.... " "	17.00	7.50	XX .... " "	9.00	4.50
" 2.... " "	15.00	7.00	French... " "	18.00	8.00
" 3.... " "	14.00	6.50	Oil Dres'd, A " "	12.50	5.50
" 4.... " "	13.00	6.00	" B " "	11.50	5.25
A...... " "	12.00	5 50	" C " "	10.50	5.00
B...... " "	10.00	5.00	" D " "	9.50	4.75
C...... " "	9.00	4 50	" E " "	8.50	4.50
D....... " "	8.00	4.00	" F " "	7.50	4.00
E........ " "	7.00	3.50			

SHEEP SKINS.

Split, A.................doz. $8.50   Plaster, A.............doz. $9.00
" B................. " 5.50   " B............. " 7.00

SUNDRIES.

Tin Ointment Boxes.

No. 1 or 1 drachm......per 100 $ .80
" 2 or 2 "   "   " .80
" 4 or ½ "   "   " 1.00
" 5 or 1 "   "   " 1.20
" 6 or 1½ "   "   " 1.40
" 7 or 2 "   "   " 1.40
" 8 or 3 "   "   " 1.50

Tin Seidlitz and Soda Boxes.

Soda..................per 100 $2.00
Seidlitz, ordinary size.. "   2.75
"   extra   " .. "   3.50

Pill Boxes, Chip and Paper.

Chip nested, round, paper.......$ .15
"   "   oval, small.....gro. .25
"   "   "   large.... "   .35
"   "   "   willow, paper.. .25

Turned Wood Boxes.

No. 1 or ⅛ oz.....gro. $ .30
" 2 or ¼ oz............ "   .40
" 3 or ½ oz............ "   .50
" 4 or 1 oz............ "   .75
" 5 or 2 oz............ " 1.00
" 6 or 3 oz............ " 1.50
" 7 or 4 oz............ " 2.00

Bougies.
                              Doz.
English, ass'd, 1 to 12........ $1.25
"   ex. large, ass'd, 1 to 20, 3.50

Catheters.
                              Doz.
English ass'd, 1 to 12......... $1.25
"   extra large ass'd, 1 to 20 3.50

Lamp Burners.
                              Doz.
Sun O.......................$1.30
" A....................... 1.40
" B....................... 2.00
Star O....................... 1.30
" A....................... 1.40
" B....................... 2.00
Hinge O....................... .85
" A....................... .95
" B....................... 1.75
Parlor....................... 1.45
Brilliant 3.50
Crystal Light................ 3.50
X. L....................... 3.00

Lamp Chimneys.
                              Doz.
Sun straight O, bbls.......... $ .35
"   "   A, " .... .36
"   "   B, " .... .50
" bulb, O, " .... .35
"   "   A, " .... .36
"   "   B, " .... .50
" scollop O, " .... .35
"   "   A, " .... .36
"   "   B, " .... .50
"   " flint O, bbls....... .50
"   "   " A, " .... .50
"   "   " B, " .... .70
" hinge   O, " .... .40
"   "   A, " .... .40
"   "   B, " .... .50
Argand No. 1............... .40
"   No. 2............... .40
Lip B....................... .55

Lamp Wicks.
                              Gro.
No. O.......................$ .35
" A....................... .40
" B....................... .70
" D....................... 1.30

Brilliant.
                              Gro.
Crystal Light................$1.60
Tom Thumb, round and flat... .25
Nos. 1 and 2, German Student. 1.10
No. O, felt................. .60
" A, felt................. .75
" B, felt................. 1.00

Nursing Bottles.
                              Doz.
Lang's Perfected............$3.00
Maw's Alexandria, green..... 2.50
"   "   white..... 4.00
" Export............. 2.50
" Wood Top, green..... 1.50
Crown "   "   " 1.25
Imperial, Alex. Pattern........ 2.00
Moulded Flask.... .... .75
"   "   wide mouth... .90

Nursing Bottle Trimmings.
                              Doz.
French (comb'n will fit any bot.) $2.00
Maw's Alexandra.............. 2.00
"   Export............ 1.75
"   Wood-Top............ .75
"   "   pure gum.... 1.00
Lang's Perfected............ 1.50
Black, American............. 1.00
White, " .... .75
Maroon, " 1.25

Nursing Bottle Cleaners.
                              Doz.
Patent....,................ $0.75
Brushes, No. 1, for bottles.. .50
" No. 2,   "   ..... .50
" for Tubes............ .25

Nipples.
                              Gross
American, small, white..... $1.50
"   medium......... 2.00
"   large " 3.00
"   small, black...... 2.00
"   medium " 3.00
"   large " 4.00
English, large.............. 5.00
"   medium........... 3.00
"   small............ 1.75
French Maroon, small........ 4.00
"   "   medium 4.50
"   "   large 6.00
"   "   extra large.... 9.00
White....................... 2.75
" large.................. 4.00
Pure Gum.................... 3.00
"   " large 3.50
White, Patent............... 3.75
Pure Gum, Patent............ 4.00
White Swan Bill............. 2.50
Pure Gum Swan Bill.......... 3.00
White Plug.................. 7.50

Nipple Shells.
                              Doz.
Glass....................... $ .75

Nipple Shields.
                              Doz.
Boxwood.................... $ .50
"   and Nipple.......... 1.25
Glass....................... 1.25
Maw's, Glass, small........ 1.50
"   " with tube........ 2.50
Nichols, with bone guard...... 1.25
Needham's, with white nipple.. 3.00
Rubber, Black............... 1.00
"   White............. .75

Filtering Paper.
                              Per Pack.
French round, No. 15, 6 inch.. $ .20
"   "   " 19, 8 " .. .25
"   "   " 25, 10 " .. .30
"   "   " 33, 13 " .. .40
"   "   " 40, 16 " .. .50
"   "   " 45, 18 " .. .60
"   "   " 50, 20 " .. .70
"   Grey.............ream 3.50
"   White........... "   4.00

SUNDRIES.

Medicated Paper.

	Case.	Doz.
Gayetty's, 50 pckgs..	$16.00..	$3.85
Star Mills, 100 " ..	18.00..	2.50
Imperial, 100 " ..	10.00..	1.30

Probangs Sponge.

	Doz.
Plain....................	$1.00
Ivory-tipped handle..........	1.50
Wire handled................	1.00
Rattan.....................	.60

Spatulas.

	Rivet Handles.	Eng. Balance.
3 inch........doz.	$2.25 ..	$2.50
4 " "	2.50 ..	2.75
5 " "	2.75 ..	3.25
6 " "	3.25 ..	3.75
7 " "	4.00 ..	4.50
8 " "	5.00 ..	5.88
9 " "	7.00 ..	7.88
10 " "	9.00 ..	9.50
11 " "	11.00 ..	14.00
12 " "	13.50 ..	20.00
Pocket Spatulas.........doz.	6.00	
Bone................... "	2.00	

Glass Syringes.

	Gro.
No. 00, Male Syr's, Met'l Cap	$7.00
" 0, " "	8.00
" 1, " "	9.00
" 2, " "	10.00
" 3, " "	12.50
" 4, " "	14.00
" 5, " "	18.00
" 6, " "	24.00
2 oz. " "	27.00
3 oz. " "	36.00
4 oz. " "	42.00
6 oz. " "	54.00
8 oz. " "	72.00

Male Syr's, corked, same price as with metal caps.

Ex. Heavy Single Paper Cases.

	Doz.
No. 0, male.................	$1.25
No. 1, "	1.25
No. 2, "	1.50
No. 3, "	1.75
No. 4, "	2.00
No. 5, "	2.25
No. 2, oz., male.............	3.50
No. 1, Fem. Syr's, Met'l Cap..	10.00
No. 2, " "	11.00
No. 3, " "	12.50
No. 4, " "	14.00
No. 5, " "	18.00
No. 6, " "	24.00
2 oz. " "	27.00
3 oz. " "	36.00
4 oz. " "	42.00
6 oz. " "	54.00
8 oz. " "	72.00

Female Syringes, corked, same price as with metal caps.

Ex. Heavy Single Paper Cases.

	Doz.
No. 1, Female............doz.	$1.50
No. 2, "	1.62
No. 3, "	1.75
No. 4, "	2.00
No. 5, "	2.25
2 oz. "	3.50
4 oz. "	7.50
	Doz.
No. 1. Womb, with bent pipe..	1.75
No. 2, " "	2.00
No. 3, " "	2.25
No. 4, " "	2.75
2 oz. " "	2.75
3 oz. " "	3.50
4 oz. " "	4.50
6 oz. " "	6.00
8 oz. " "	7.50

2 oz. Womb, with bent pipe, glass shield......................$6.00 (Doz.)
4 oz. ditto, ditto................. 7.50
6 oz. " 9.00
Womb Syringes, corked, same price as with metal caps.

	Doz.
Ear Syr's. bent or straight,...	$1.25
Dentist Syringes.............	1.25
Eye "	1.25
Nasal " straight.......	2.00
" " curved........	3.00
Suppository Syringes, Rectum, assorted sizes.............	1.25

Metal Syringes.

	Doz.
8 oz. self, in case..........	$11.00
6 oz. "	9.00
4 oz. "	7.00
16 oz. "	16.00
12 oz. "	14.00
24 oz. "	25.00
24 oz. single, in paper boxes..	18.00
16 oz. "	12.00
12 oz. "	10.00
10 oz. "	9.00
8 oz. "	7.00
6 oz. "	5.00
4 oz. "	4.00
2 oz. "	3.00
1 oz. "	2.50
P. P. "	1.00
Horse, metal, 24 oz.........	30.00
" 36 oz.........	36.00
" 48 oz.........	48.00

Rubber Syringes, Bulb.

	Doz.
Davidson's met. pipes,&c. No. 1.	$16.00
" " 2	13.00
" hard rub. pipes, etc., No. 4...................	18.00
Delano, No. 502..............	6.00
" No. 505	7.50
" No. 506	7.00
" No. 507	6.00
Mattson's Anglo-American....	7.00
" Family.......	17.00
" New-York.......	5.00
" Jet and Spray....	9.00
" Original.......	9.00
New-York, No. 1	10.50
" No. 2...........	7.50
" No. 3...........	4.50
" No. 4...........	3.75

Thermometers.

TIN CASE, Japanned.

	Doz.
7 inch....................	$2.50
8 "	2.75
10 "	3.00
12 "	4.00

DAIRY.

	Doz.
7 inch....................	$2.50
8 "	3.00
10 "	3.50

SOLID BLACK-WALNUT.

	Doz.
8 inch, square ends........	$6.00
10 " "	8.00

Tooth-Picks.

Quill, No. 3, small...per 1000, $ .80
" " 4, medium. " 1.25
" " 5, large.... " 1.50
Wood, 2500 in box, case 100 bxs. 7.50

Tubing.

	Foot.
India Rubber, 1-16 inch, white	$ .05
" " 1/8 " "	.06
" " 3-16 " "	.09
" " 1/4 " "	.12
" " 3/8 " "	.16
" " 1/2 " "	.18
" " 5/8 " "	.21
" " 3/4 " "	.20
" " 1 " "	.35

Twines.

	Doz.
Cotton, Sea Island, assorted..	$ .50
" " " pink......	.75
" " " bulk......	.50

LAUDANUM.

Small panel vials..doz. $ .70	½ pint panel bots..doz. $2.25
Med. " " ..doz. .90	Pint " " ..doz. 4.00
Large " " ..doz. 1.50	Quart " " ..doz. 7.50
Packed 2 doz. in wood boxes.	Packed 1 doz. in wood boxes.

PAREGORIC.

Small panel vials..doz. .50	½ pint panel bots..doz. 1.50
Med. " " ..doz. .60	Pint " " ..doz. 2.50
Large " " ..doz. 1.00	Quart " " ..doz. 4.50
Packed 2 doz. in wood boxes.	Packed 1 doz. in wood boxes.

CASTOR OIL.

Med. panel vials..doz. .50	½ pint panel bots..doz. 1.25
Large " " ..doz. .75	Pint " " ..doz. 2.00
Packed 2 doz. in wood boxes.	Quart " " ..doz. 3.50
	Packed 1 doz. in wood boxes.

SWEET OIL.

Med. panel vials..doz. .50	½ pint panel bots..doz. 1.00
Large " " ..doz. .70	Pint " " ..doz. 1.75
Packed 2 doz. in wood boxes.	Quart " " ..doz. 3.00
	Packed 1 doz. in wood boxes.

ESSENCES.

Essence Lemon, Peppermint, Wintergreen, Cinnamon, Cloves.

Small panel vials..doz. .55	½ pint panel bots..doz. 1.75
Med. " " ..doz. .65	Pint " " ..doz. 3.00
Large " " ..doz. 1.10	Quart " " ..doz. 5.25
Packed 2 doz. in wood boxes.	Packed 1 doz. in wood boxes.

SPIRITS.

Spirits Niter, Camphor, Lavender Comp.

Small panel vials..doz. .55	½ pint panel bots..doz. 1.75
Med. " " ..doz. .65	Pint " " ..doz. 3.00
Large " " ..doz. 1.10	Quart " " ..doz. 5.25
Packed 2 doz. in wood boxes.	Packed 1 doz. in wood boxes.

SPIRITS TURPENTINE.

Small panel vials ..doz. .30	½ pint panel bots..doz. .90
Med. " " ..doz. .40	Pint " " ..doz. 1.50
Large " " ..doz. .60	Quart " " ..doz. 2.50
Packed 2 doz. in wood boxes.	Packed 1 doz. in wood boxes.

SYRUPS.

Syrup Squills, Squills Comp. (Hive Syrup), Ipecac, Rhei.

Small panel vials..doz. .50	½ pint panel bots..doz. 1.25
Med. " " ..doz. .60	Pint " " ..doz. 2.50
Large " " ..doz. 1.00	Quart " " ..doz. 4.50
Packed 2 doz. in wood boxes.	Packed 1 doz. in wood boxes.

Discount 10% 1 Gross Lots.

S. R. VAN DUZER,

Sole Agent for United States.

BRIDAL BOUQUET BLOOM,

For Beautifying the Complexion.

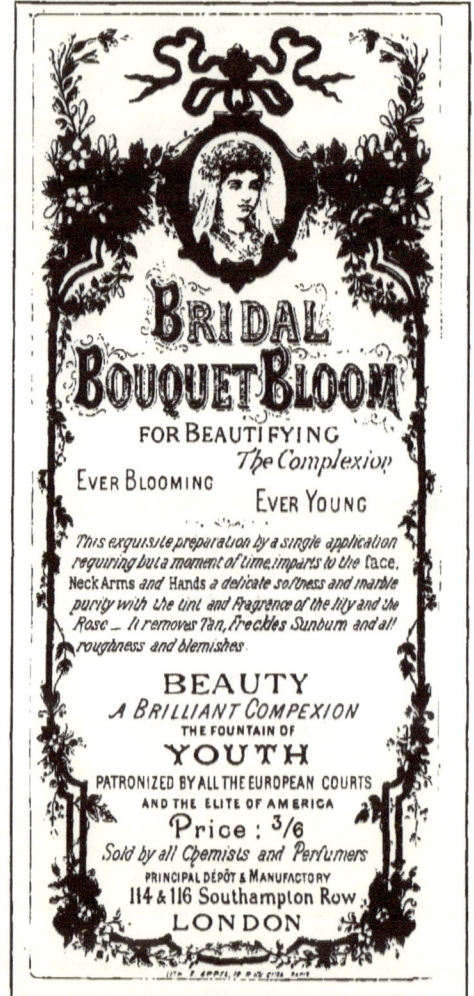

S. R. VAN DUZER,

Sole Agent for United States.

FLORAL BELL FRAGRANT ELIXIR OR LIQUID DENTIFRICE.

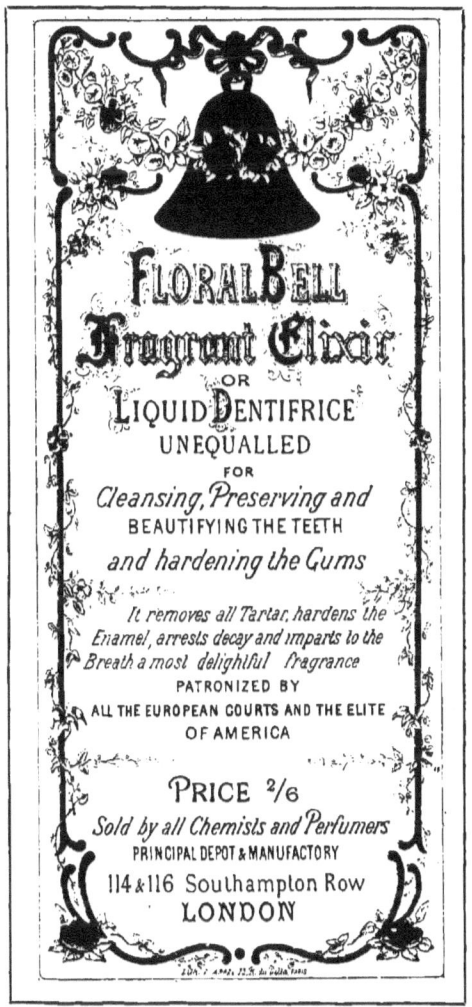

Trade Prices.

FLORAL BELL FRAGRANT ELIXIR.

Each bottle is enclosed in an elegant card-board case.

Floral Bell Fragrant Elixir...............per gross	$66.00
Floral Bell Fragrant Elixir...............per dozen	6.00
Floral Bell Fragrant Elixir...............per bottle	0.75

*The price noted on the above fac-simile label is the sterling price
for Great Britain.*

PATENT MEDICINES AND PROPRIETARY ARTICLES.

	Doz.	Gross.
Acid, Phosphates, Hosford's small	$4.00	....
" " " large	8.00	....
Alterative, Jayne's	7.60	...
Ambrosia, Ring's	6.25	...
Annihilator, Hedges, F. & A.	7.75	....
" Wolcott's Pain, small	1.75	....
" " " medium	3.50	....
" " " large	7.00	....
Anodyne, Hunnewell's Tolu	3.50	....
" Townsley's T. A.	1.60	.. .
Anti-Fat, Allen's	10.75	....
Aperient, Tarrant's Seltzer	8.00	....
August Flower, Green's, trial size	.85	$9.50
" " "	5.50	63.00
Axle Grease	.75	7.50
Balm, Hagan's Magnolia	5.25	60.00
" Miller's Magnetic	1.85	21.00
Balsam, Allen's Lung	7.00	81.00
" Arnold's, Seth, Diarrhœa	1.90	....
" Blackman's, small	2.65	....
" Blackman's, large	5.25	....
" Coe's Cough, small	2.75	...
" Fitch's Pulmonary	8.50	...
" Hall's Lung	7.50	....
" Hill's, of Honey	1.00	9.00
" Hyatt's Infallible Life	8.00	....
" " " " A. B., double	11.50	...
" " Pulmonic Life	7.75	....
" Jayne's Carminative, small	2.85	...
" " " large	3.80	....
" Keating's Horehound, small	1.65	....
" Miller's	3.85	....
" Porter's, Madame, small	1.90	21.60
" " " medium	3.80	43.20
" " " large	5.70	64.80
" Roman Eye	1.75	19.50
" Seabury's Cough, small	1.85	21.00
" " " large	3.65	42.00
" Turlington's	.75	8.00
" Van Deusen's Cough	2.75	30.00
" Wistar's Wild Cherry. small	4.00	47.00
" " " " large	8.00	93.00
Barley, Robinson's Patent, 1 lb. papers	1.25	13.50
Bellows, Insect, small	1.75	....
Bay Rum, Hock bottles, S. R. V. D. & Co's, qts.	6.75	....
" " " " pts.	4.50	...
" " " " ½ pts.	3.00	....
Benzine, Hegeman's	1.25	13.50
" Roland's	.85	9.00
Bitters, Angostura, Genuine	9.00	....
" Atwood's Jaundice	1.60	16.50
" Boker's Stomach	12.50	....
" Drake's Plantation	8.38	99.00
" Hoofland's German	8.00	93.00
" Hop	7.25	84.00
" Hostetter's Stomach	8.38	99.00
" Langley's, small	2.75	...
" " medium	5.50	...
" " large	7.00	...
" Mishler's Herb	8.00	93.00
" Porter's, Madame, small	1.90	21.60
" " " large	3.80	43.20
" Walker's Vinegar	8.25	....
Bloom of Youth, Laird's	5.25	....
Bloom "Bridal Bouquet"	5.25	57.00
Blacking, Royal, No. 1	....	2.75
" " " 2	....	3.25
" " " 3	....	4.00
" " " 4	....	5.50

	Doz.	Gross.
Bluing, S. R. V. D. & Co's, small pepper-box style, improved tin top		$2.00
" S. R. V. D. & Co's, large pepper-box style, improved tin top	....	3.00
" S. R. V. D. & Co's, small flat box style..	....	2.25
" " " large flat " " ..	....	3.25
" " " 2 oz. bots., 3 doz. bxs.	....	3.50
" " " 4 oz. " 3 doz. bxs.	....	4.75
" " " 8 oz. " 3 doz. bxs.	.. .	7.00
" " " 12 oz. " 3 doz. bxs.	....	10.75
" " " 16 oz. " 1 doz. bxs.	....	14.00
" " " 32 oz. " 1 doz. bxs.	....	25.00
Borax, Smith's, 1 lb. papers	$1.75	....
" " ½ lb. "	1.00	....
Bromo-Chloralum. Tilden's	3.75	....
Cakes, Yeast, National 3 doz. cases.	.62	....
" " Twin Brothers 3 " "	.62	....
" " Yankee 3 " "	.60	....
Bronchials, Brown's	1.50	...
Camphorine, Hoyt's..	1.75	20.00
Capsules, Dundas, Dick & Co's, Balsam Copaiba.	2.50	....
" " " Castor Oil	3.00	....
" " " Cod Liv. Oil	3.00	....
" " " " with Io. Iron	4.00	....
" " " Copaiba & Oil Cub..	6.00	....
" " " Matico Cub. & Cop.	7.00	....
" " " Oil Male Fern	5.00	....
" " " " Sandal Wood...	12.00	....
" " " " Turpentine	3.00	....
" Mathey-Caylus' Capsules of Copaiba ; Cop. and Cub. ; Cop. and Citrate of Iron ; Cop. and Rhatany ; Cop. Cub. and Rhatany ; Cop. Cub. and Carb. of Iron ; Cop. Cub. and Alum ; Cop. and Magnesia ; Cop. and Catechu ; Cop. and Subnit. of Bismuth ; Cop. and Tannic Acid ; Cop. and Tar ; Cop. Pepsine and Bismuth ; Cob. and Alum ; Cub. and Turpentine ; Cub. and Tannate of Iron ; Venice Turpentine ; Norway Tar	6.75	
Cop. and Oil of Sandal Wood ; Cop. Cub. and Oil of Sandal Wood ; Cop. Iron and Sandal Wood	9.00	....
Capsules, Planten's Castor Oil, No. 1	1.25	....
" " " " " 2	2.25	....
" " " " " 3	3.25	....
" " Cod Liver Oil, No. 3	3.00	....
" " Copaiba, No. 1	1.00	....
" " " " 2	1.75	....
" " " " 3	2.50	....
" " Cop. & Cub. " 1	1.50	....
" " " " 2	2.90	....
" " " " 3	4.00	....
" " Empty	3.00	....
" " Oil Sandal Wood	9.00	....
Carboline	7.25	84.00
Carminative, Dalby's Am	1.25	13.50
" Jayne's, small	2.85	....
" " large	3.80	..
Castoria, Pitchers	2.75	31.50
Catholicon, Marchisi's	12.50	....
" Marshall's	8.50	....
Cement, Edes' Diamond	1.50	....
" Van Stan's Stratena	1.25	13.50
Cerate, Weaver's	2.85	....
Chewing Gum, Adams', India Rubber....box, 30	....	....
" " Curtis' Spruce, in lumps..box, 75	....	.....
" " " " in sticks..box, 50	....	....
Chlorodyne, Brown's, small	4.25	....
Cholagogue, Osgood's	12.50	...
Cloverine, small	1.25	13.50
Cocoaine, Burnett's.	7.50	87.00
Color, Perfected Butter, W. R. & Co's, Sample..	.60	...
" " " " " " Small ...	1.90	22.50

	Doz.	Gross.
Color, Perfected Butter, W. R. & Co's, Medium.	$3.80	$45.00
" " " " " " Large ...	8.00	93.00
Comfits, Brown's Worm.......................	1.55	17.50
Compound, Clark's Anti-bilious	7.50	....
" Poland's White Pine	7.50	....
Confections, Holloway's Worm................	1.50	16.00
" Van Deusen's Worm..............	1.50	16.50
Cordial, Brown's Teething	1.50	....
" Fosgate's...........	2.75	....
" Godfrey's....................	.65	6.00
" McLean's	8.25	99.00
" Wishart's Pine Tree..	7.50	....
Corrector, Fitch's Biliary, small............	4.50	....
" " " large............	8.50	....
" " Heart, small	6.50	...
" " " large............	13.00	....
Cosmoline, Houghton's, Plain, small..........	2.00	21.00
" " " large.	3.50	36.00
" " Rose, Perfumed, small..	2.00	21.00
" " " large..	3.50	36.00
Cream, Gouraud's Oriental..................	12.00	....
Crystals, Washing, Fisher's.................	1.50	....
Cubebs, Marshall's Prepared	1.90	21.00
Cure, Ayer's Ague.......................	7.88	94.00
" Coe's Dyspepsia	7.50	87.00
" Guild's G. M. Asthma	11.00	....
" Himrod's Asthma.................	7.50	84.00
" Jayne's Ague	7.60	....
" Knapp's Throat....................	2.75	30.00
" Piso's Consumption, small.........	2.00	....
" " " large........	7.50	...
" Sanford's Radical.....................	8.25	96.00
" Upham's Asthma..................	3.75	....
" Wei de Meyers' Catarrh...........	12.00	....
Cuticle, Judd's Liquid.	2.25	....
Cuticura, small................	4.25	....
" large....................	8.50	....
" Resolvent	8.50	....
" Soap	2.50	....
Dead Shot, Dutcher's, for Bugs, small.........	1.85	21.00
" " Peery's, for Worms...........	1.65	....
Dermador, Anderson's, small................	1.85	21.00
" " large..............	3.70	42.00
Discovery, Kennedy's Medical....	12.50	....
" Pierce's Medical..............	7.50	88.00
Disinfectant, Girondin, quarts......	4.00	....
Dissolvent, Kennedy's Rheumatic.............	12.50	....
Dressing, Brown's French.....................	.90	10.00
Drops, Bateman's........................	.75	8.00
" Brummell's Cough................	1.20	13.50
" Marshall's Pine Tree Tar	1.75	....
" Pike's Toothache	1.62	18.00
" Townley's Toothache.....	1.62	18.00
" Wishart's Worm........... ...	1.50	16.00
Dye Colors, Handy Package..................	1.00	....
" " Leamon's	1.65	18.00
" " " trial size..............	.88	9.50
" " Star................ ...	1.65	....
Electro Silicon......	1.10	12.00
Elixir, Down's, small....................	2.75	30.00
" McMunn's, of Opium...............	3.35	40.00
" Tilden's Iodo Brom. Calc. Co..........	10.50	120.00
" Wheeler's Calisaya and Phosphates......	8.00	90.00
Essence, Coffee, Hummel's, in foil.......	....	2.50
" " " in tin	....	3.75
" Ginger, Brown's.................	3.65	43.00
" " Williams, small.............	1.75	20.00
" " S. R. V. D. & Co's..........	3.25	36.00
" " Roland's...................	1.75	20.00
Expectorant, Jayne's	7.60	....
Exterminator, Costar's Rat, small	1.35	15.00
" " " large..............	2.75	30.00
" Parson's	1.25	....
Extract Buchu, Helmbold's.................	7.75	...
" " and Iron, Rush's..............	7.75	....
" Cubebs and Copaiva, Tarrant's........	8.00	....

	Doz.	Gross.
Extract Dandelion, Brewer's	$1.75	....

" Flavoring, S. R. V. D. & Co's Fruit Brand, Standard Quality.

Lemon, Almond, Orange, and all others			
	2 oz.	2.00	$24.00
	5 oz.	4.00	48.00
	10 oz.	8.00	96.00
	pints,	15.50	....
	quarts,	30.00	....
Vanilla	2 oz.	3.00	36.00
	5 oz.	6.00	72.00
	10 oz.	12.00	144.00
	pints,	24.50	....
	quarts,	43.00	....

Discount, 15 per cent.

" Flavoring, " Lupin's."

Lemon, Almond, Orange, and all others			
	2 oz.	1.50	18.00
	5 oz.	3.00	36.00
	10 oz.	6.00	72.00
	pints,	11.00	
	quarts,	21.00	....
Vanilla	2 oz.	1.75	21.00
	5 oz.	3.50	42.00
	10 oz.	7.00	84.00
	pints,	13.00	
	quarts,	25.00	....

Discount, 15 per cent.

" Flavoring, " Roland's."

" Lemon and all flavors except Vanilla, small size only	1.00	12.00
" Vanilla....... " " "	1.25	15.00

Discount, 15 per cent.

	Doz.	Gross.
" . Malt, Hoff's	3.50	39.00
" " Trommer's. with Hops (Plain)	7.50	....
" " " with Pyrophos. of Iron (Fer.)	7.50	..
" " " with Cod Liver Oil	7.50	....
" " " with Hypophosphites	10.50	....
" Roots, Dutcher's, for Beer	1.75	....
" " Knapp's, for Beer, small	1.85	21.00
" " " " " medium	3.70	42.00
" " " " " large	7.40	84.00
" " " " " quarts	26.00	....
" Smartweed, Pierce's	3.75	44.00
" Witch Hazel, bulk..........gall., 1.25		....
" " " Pond's, small	3.75	....
" " " " medium	7.50	....
" " " " large	15.00	....
Farina, Hecker's, 1 lb. papers, bxs. 48 lbs. box, 4.50	....	....
" " ½ lb. " " 24 lbs. box, 2.35	...	....
Floral Bell or Fragrant Elixir	6.00	66.00
Food, Nestle's Lacteous	4.75	....
Friend, Clotwerthy's Poulterers'	1.50	....
Fumigators, Perrin's, small	1.62	19.00
" " large	7.50	....
Gelatine, Cox's	1.65	18.50
" Nelson's	1.60	18.00
Ginger, Sanford's Jamaica	3.35	....
Glue, Spalding's	1.65	19.00
Glue-Pots, Muchmore's	1.85	....
Guns, Lyons' Powder	2.25	....
" Roland's "	1.50	....
Hair Balsam, Parker's, small	4.00	45.00
" " " large	7.00	78.00
" Dye, Batchelor's, small	7.50	...
" " " medium	10.50	....
" " " large	23.00	....
" " Buckingham's Whisker	3.75	....
" " Cristadoro's, small	7.50	....
" " Hill's	3.75	....
" " Jayne's	8.50	....
" " Miller's	3.75	....
" Renewer, Hall's Sicilian	6.75	80.00
" Restorer, Allen's, Mrs. S. A.	10.00	112.00
" Tonic, Jayne's	7.60	....
" Vigor, Ayer's	6.75	79.00
Honey, Horehound, and Tar, Hale's, small	3.87	45.00
" " " " large	7.75	90.00

	Doz.	Gross.
Honey, Liverwort, Nowill's..................	$2.50	....
Imperial Granum, small	5.75	$67.00
" " large	9.50	....
Ink, Indelible, Payson's	2.00	22.50
" " Tarrant's..................	2.75	....

BLACK, BLUE, VIOLET.

	Doz.	Gross.
" S. R. V. D. & Co's Stands......3 doz. bxs.	.40	4.50
" " " 4 oz...........1 doz. bxs.	1.00	10.00
" " " 6 oz...........1 doz. bxs.	1.25	13.00
" " " 8 oz...........1 doz. bxs.	1.50	16.00
" " " Pints ....1 doz. bxs.	2.75	28.00
" " " Quarts.......1 doz. bxs.	4.50	48.00
" " " Jugs..........1 gallon.	18.00	....
" " " Monitor or nosed.3 doz. bxs.	.30	3.25
Invigorator, Sanford's Liver.............	8.00	93.00
Juice, Valentine's Meat......................	8.25	....
" " " with Glycerine.........	4.00	....
Kalliston, Burnett's........................	7.50	87.00
Kathairon, Lyon's..........................	3.75	42.00
Killer, Arnold's, Seth, Cough, small...........	1.75	20.00
" " " " medium	3.50	40.00
" Flagg's Cough, small..................	3.75	....
" " " large...	7.50	....
" Laycock's Worm....................	1.60	18.00
Lactopeptine, 1 oz. vials......	8.00	90.00
Life for the Hair, Chevalier's.............	6.50	75.00
Liniment, Burdsall's Arnica	3.00	34.50
" Centaur (White or Yellow), trinl......	1.85	21.00
" " " " small.....	3.75	42.00
" " " " large.....	7.50	84.00
" Giles' Iodide Am., Fam. or Horse, trial.	1.85	21.00
" " " " " " sml .	3.75	42.00
" " " " " " large	7.50	84.00
" " " " " " qts	22.50	....
" Herrick's German Horse, small......	3.75	42.00
" " " " large......	7.50	84.00
" Hunt's..........................	3.50	39.00
" Jadwin's Subduing, small............	1.85	21.00
" " " large............	3.75	42.00
" " " Horse............	7.50	84.00
" Jayne's	3.80	....
" Kennedy's Rheumatic.............	3.87	45.00
" " Scattering	7.75	90.00
" Low's Magnetic....................	3.00	....
" Mathis' Family.........	1.50	16.50
" Mexican Mustang, small.............	1.85	21.00
" " " medium	3.70	42.00
" " " large.............	7.50	84.00
" Sweet's, small......................	3.00	....
" " large	6.00	....
" Tobias' Venetian, small..............	2.00	....
" " " large..........	4.00	....
" " " Horse	7.50	....
" Wells'	2.75	....
" Young America....................	1.50	16.00
Lotion, Perry's Moth and Freckle...........	13.00	....
Magnesia, Citrate, Solution, Ellis'.............	2.25	24.00
" " Dry, Ellis'...............	3.00	.. ..
" " Granulated, Ellis'..........	3.75	....
" " Eng. granulated	3.00	33.00
" " Rogers'....................	2.75	....
" " Solution, S. R. V. D. & Co's..	2.00	22.00
" Husband's Calcined	3.00	34.50
Matches, "Special Safety," S. R. V. D. & Co's, 100's..........5 and 10 gross cases.		2.50
" "Special Safety," S. R. V. D. & Co's, 300's.............3½ gross cases.		7.35
" Sulph., No. 2, ¼'s..5 and 10 gross cases.		2.35
" " 2, ⅛'s..5 and 10 gross cases.		2.30
" Parlor, Swift & Courtney's, 80's...... 5 and 10 gross cases.		2.70
" Parlor, Swift & Courtney's, 60's .... 5 and 10 gross cases.		2.40
" Parlor, Swift & Courtney's, 500's...... 1 gross cases.		14.00

	Doz.	Gross.
Matches, Parlor, Swift & Courtney's, 300's......		
2 gross cases.	....	$8.40
" Parlor, Swift & Courtney's, round bxs .		
5 and 10 gross cases.		2.80
Milk, Condensed, Anglo-Swiss Co.		
Prepared in England.........4 doz. case.	$5.75	
" " Cham, Switz ....4 " "	6.75	
Milk, Condensed, Borden's.		
Eagle ....4 " "	8.00	....
Crown...................4 " "	6.00	....
" of Magnesia, Philips', small.	3.87	45.00
" " " " large........... ...	7.75	90.00
Mucilage, S. R. V. D. & Co's, 3 oz., cap. 1 doz. bxs.	1.00	9.00
" " " ½ pts....1 doz. bxs.	3.50	39.00
" " " pts....1 doz. bxs.	5.00	54.00
" " " qts....1 doz. bxs.	9.00	96.00
Oil, Cod-Liver, De Jongh's...................	7.00	....
" " " Fougera's...................	11.50	....
" " " Hazard & Caswell's	6.50	....
" " " Hegeman's...................	6.50	....
" " " Marvin's...................	6.50	....
" " " Moller's	5.50	....
" " " Phillips', with Phospho-Nutritine.	7.50	....
" " " S. R. V. D. & Co's, full size, in bots	5.75	66.00
" " " " " half " "	3.25	36.00
" " " and Lime, Scott's..............	7.50	87.00
" " " " " Wilbor's............	8.50	....
" Green Mountain, small...................	1.75	....
" " " large.	3.50	....
" Hamlin's Wizard, small.	3.75	42.00
" " " large...................	7.50	84.00
" Harlem, Genuine...................	.75	6.00
" " Sylvester's	3.25	....
" Hoofland's Greek, small...................	3.75	....
" " " large...................	7.50	....
" Merchant's Gargling, small...............	1.90	22.50
" " " medium	3.85	45.00
" " " large.........	7.70	90.00
" Miller's Harness, ½ pts.................	1.75	....
" " " No. 1.................	3.50	....
" " " " 2.................	5.50	....
" Renne's Magic, small.....	1.85	21.00
" " " medium	3.75	42.00
" " " large...............	7.50	84.00
" Sewing Machine, S. R. V. D. & Co's	1.00	10.00
Ointment, Brown's O. P., Herbal, small........	2.00	21.60
" " " " large........	4.00	43.20
" Graefenberg, Green Mountain.... .	1.60	18.00
" Heiskell's Tetter..............	3.75	42.00
" Holloway's, small..............	1.75	18.00
" " medium	4.50	....
" " large	8.00	....
" Kennedy's Healing................	3.87	45.00
" " Hemlock	4.00	....
" " Salt Rheum.....	3.87	45.00
" " Scrofula	7.75	90.00
" McAllister's	1.65	19.00
" Miner's Botanic, small....	1.75	19.50
" Tanner's German...................	1.75	19.50
" Trask's Magnetic, small..............	1.85	21.00
" " " large	2.85	33.00
Olive Tar, Stafford's........................	3.75	44.00
Opodeldoc, Liquid....................	1.00	10.50
" Steers'	1.00	10.50
Pads, Holman's Fever and Ague..............	16.00	....
Pain-Killer, Perry Davis', small..............	1.85	22.00
" " " medium	3.75	42.50
" " " large	7.50	85.00
Panacea, Baker's Pain, small................	1.85	22.00
" Curtis & Brown's Household.........	1.85	....
" Swaim's	18.00	194.00
Paper, Fly, Dutcher's.............per ream, 7.50		
" " Isaacsen's Sticky.....per 100, 2.00		
" " Stayner's " .....per 100, 2.00		
Pectoral, Ayer's Cherry....................	7.88	94.00
Pepsin, Am., Hawley's Aromat'd,1 oz.bts.oz., .45		

Doz. Gross.

Pepsin, Am., Hawley's Sacch., 1 lb. bots. lb., $6.00			
" " " " ½ lb. " .lb., 6.10			
" " " " ¼ lb. " .lb., 6.20			
" " " " 1 oz. " .oz., .45			
" " Scheffer's Sacch., 1 oz. " .oz., .60			
" French, Boudalt's, 1 oz. " .oz., .80			
Phosphates, Percy's Vitalized	$8.25	....
Pills, Ayer's S. C.	1.50	$17.50
" Arnold's	1.50	15.00
" Blair's Gout, small	5.50	....
" " " large	9.25	....
" Blancard's, small	5.00	....
" " large	9.00	....
" Brandreth's	1.25	14.00
" " S. C	1.25	14 00
" Bristol's	1.50	....
" Brown's O. P., small	2.00	21.60
" " " large	4.00	43.20
" Clarke's Female	7.50	87.00
" Deshler's Fever and Ague	7.50	90.00
" Filkins'	1.35	15.00
" Graefenberg	1.40	15.50
" Herrick's	1.50	17.00
" Holloway's, small	1.75	....
" " medium	4.50	....
" " large	8.00	...
" Hoofland's	1.75	19.50
" Hooper's American	.50	4.50
" Jayne's Sanative	1.65	....
" Lee's, Windham	1.35	15.00
" McLane's Liver	1.50	17.25
" McLean's, J. H., Universal	1.25	14.00
" " " Chinoidine	7.00	78.00
" Moffat's	1.50	16.00
" Mott's Liver	1.50	17.00
" Parson's Purgative	1.50	....
" Pierce's Purgative Pellets	1.70	19.50
" Porter's	1.50	16.50
" Radway's	1.50	17.50
" Schenck's Mandrake	1.50	....
" Shallenberger's, F. & A	7.50	....
" Sholl's Fever and Ague	3.50	....
" Tallcott's Magic, small	3.75	....
" " " large	7.50	....
" Tutt's Liver	1.50	17.00
" Van Deusen's	1.50	....
" Wright's Indian Vegetable, Plain	1.42	16.00
" " " " S. C	1.50	17.00
Pilules, Moore's	3.75	42.00
Plasters, Allcock's Porous	1.20	13.50
" " " Yard rolls	18.00	. ..
" Benson's Capcine	1.75	20.00
" Coddington's Capsicum, sml. 1 yard rolls	6.00	....
" " " lge. 2 " "	12.00	...
" Collins' Voltaic	1.85	21.00
" Crew's Mustard, No. 1	.75	....
" " " 2	.88	....
" " " 3	1.00	....
" Crittenton's P. M. Cloth, No. 1	.75	....
" " " " 2	1 00	....
" " " " 3	1.25	.. .
" " " Kid, 1	1.00	....
" " " " 2	1.25	....
" " " " 3	2.00	....
" Grosvenor's Arnica, No. 1	.85	10.00
" " Belladonna, No. 1	1.25	15.00
" " " 1 yard rolls	11.00	....
" " Porous	1.00	....
" Herrick's Strengthening	1.37	16.00
" " Perforated	1.12	12.00
" " Capsicum	1.12	12.00
" Holloway's Arnica, small	1.00	11.00
" " " medium	1.10	16.50
" " " large	2.00	22.00
" Isinglass, Husband's, No. 1, yard rolls.	6.50	....
" Montauk Porous	.75	8.00

	Doz.	Gross.
Plasters, Rigollot's Mustard, in boxes of 10....	$3.25	. . .
" " " " " 25...	7.50	....
" " " " " 100 ...	30.00	....
" Seabury & Johnson's Bella., porous.. .	1.13	....
" " " " 1 yard rolls..	7.20	...
" " " " strengthening	1.00	....
Polish, Bro. Jonathan's Furniture............ .	2.25	
" Dixon's Stove.......................	.55	$5.25
" Silver Luster Stove.................	.50	3.50
" Star Plate	3.50	
Powders, Condition, Foutz's..................	1.50	17.50
" " Fronefield's..............	1.35	15.50
" " Harvell's, small	1.40	16.00
" . " " large	3.35	39.00
" " Punderson's	1.50	17.00
" " Sheridan's....	1.50	17.00
" " Tobias' Derby......	1.60	18.00
" Insect, Costar's....................	1.35	15.00
". " Isaacsen's	1.50	17.00
" " Knowles', small... .:......	1.75	20.00
" " " medium	3.50	40.00
". " " large.............	7.00	80.00
" " Lyons' Magnetic	1.85	21.00
" " Roland's...................	....	18.00
" Iron and Sulphur. Stafford's.........	7.25	87.00
" Seidlitz, S. R. V. D. & Co's, full weight.	3.00	33.00
" " " " extra......	3.50	39.00
" Soda, "	1.50	16.50
". Yeast, Gantz's. Sea Foam...........	2.90	....
" Baking, S. R. V. D. & Co's Perfection,		
1/4 lb. tins, 3 doz. boxes....		13.20
" " S. R. V. D. & Co's Perfection,		
1/2 lb. tins, 2 doz. boxes....		24.00
" " S. R. V. D. & Co's Perfection,		
1 lb. tins, 1 doz boxes....	....	45.00
" " Royal, 1/4 lb. tins, 3 doz. bxs..	1.40	....
" " " 1/2 lb. " 2 " " ..	2.60	....
" " " 1 lb. " .2 " " ..	5.00	....
Prairie Weed, Kennedy's..............	7.75	90.00
Preparation, Hosford's Bread, 3 doz. boxes..box.	6.25	....
Prescription, Pierce's Favorite	11.00	....
Preservative, Miller's, Frank, Leather, No. 1...	1.00	....
" " " " " 2..	1.50	....
Regulator, Simmons' Liver, Dry............ ..	7.00	....
" " " " small..........	2.00	....
" " " Liquid	7.00	....
" " " " small........	4.00	....
Relief, Radway's Ready......................	3.75	44.00
Remedy, Kennedy's Favorite..................	8.00	93.00
" Sage's Catarrh......	3.50	39.00
" Mathis' Dysentery............... ..	1.50	16.50
" Sanford's Catarrh...................	8.50	....
" Van Deusen's Ready........	2.00	....
" Whitcomb's Asthma.................	11.50	....
Rennet, Shinn's.............................	1.50	....
" Wyeth's.............................	1.50	....
Resolvent, Radway's	8.50	99.00
Salt, German Bathing, 1 lb. boxes.............	.84	9.50
Salve, Blackman's.	1.50	....
" Conklin's............................	.75	7.50
" Dalley's, small........................	1.87	21.00
" " large.........................	3.75	42.00
" " Horse.........................	3.75	42.00
" Griswold's	1.65	18.00
" Henry's Carbolic......................	1.75	20.00
" Page's Climax........................	1.85	21.00
" Peleg White's, small..................	.75	7.50
" " " large....................	1.50	16.50
". Pettit's Eye	1.60	
" Raymond's Arnica	1.25	..
" Redding's Russia......................	1.85	21.00
" Sawyer's, Mrs........................	3.87	.. .
" " " small	2.00	...
" Smith's Magnetic.....................	1.50	16.50
Sapolio, Morgan's Hand, small................	....	6.00
" " " large	....	10.00

	Doz.	Gross.
Sapolio, Morgan's Hand, Polishing	$ .87	$10.00
Sarsaparilla, Ayer's	7.88	94.00
" Bristol's	10.00	....
" Bull's, John	8.00	...
" and Iron, Rush's	7.75	....
" Townsend's, Old Dr	9.00	....
" " S. P	9.00	....
Sauce, Pepper, pints	1.25	....
" " quarts	1.75	....
Schnapps, Wolfe's, pints	5.25	60.00
" " quarts	9.50	108.00
Sea Salt, Ditman's, small	1.65	18.00
" " medium	3.25	36.00
" " large	6.50	72.00
" Tidman's, boxes, 7 lbs	5.50	....
Snuff, Durno's Catarrh	1.75	....
" Marshall's Catarrh	1.75	....
Sozodont, Van Buskirk's	6.00	69.00
Specifics, Humphrey's, Nos. 1 to 15, inclusive	1.75	19.50
" " 16 to 27, "	3.50	39.00
" " 29, 30, 31, 34, 35	3.50	39.00
" " 28, 32, 33	6.00	...
Syrup, Boschee's German	5.50	63.00
" " " sample	.85	9.60
" Bull's Cough, small	2.00	21.00
" " " medium	4.00	42.00
" " " large	8.00	90.00
" Bumstead's Worm	1.50	....
" Peruvian, small	8.00	93.00
" " large	16.00	....
" Clark Johnson's Indian Blood, small	3.75	42.00
" " " " large	7.50	84.00
" Corbin's Worm	1.50	16.50
" Edwards' W. C. and Tar, small	1.50	16.50
" " " " medium	3.00	33.00
" " " " large	6.00	66.00
" Fellows' Hypophosphites, Compound	11.50	....
" Low's Worm	1.50	17.00
" Mother Noble's Healing, small	4.20	46.00
" " " " large	8.40	92.00
" Ransom's Hive	2.50	27.00
" Reuter's Life	8.25	....
" Rogers' Liv. Tar and Can	7.50	87.00
" " Worm	1.75	20.00
" Schenck's Pulmonic	8.25	96.00
" Scovill's Blood and Liver	7.50	87.00
" Seabury's Hive	1.85	21.00
" Tobias' Pulmonic	4.00	....
" Weaver's Salt Rheum	10.25	..
" Winchester's Hypophos., small	7.50	....
" " " large	15.00	....
" " " and Manganese	8.00	....
" Winslow's Soothing	1.85	21.00
" Wood's " small	1.75	....
" " " large	3.50	....
Tamar Indien	7.50	....
Tea, Hamburg, Freese & Co's	1.85	....
" Judson's Worm	1.50	....
" Kellogg's Worm	1.65	....
" Koenig's Hamburg Breast	1.75	....
" Quirk's Irish	1.75	....
" Webber's Alpine	1.50	....
" " Hamburg	1.50	....
Thermaline, small	2.00	22.50
" medium	3.75	42.00
Tincture, Norwood's Ver. Viride	12.00	....
Tonic, Hoofland's German	12.00	....
" Parker's Ginger, small	4.00	45.00
" " " large	8.00	90.00
" " " sample bots	1.20	13.00
" Schenck's Sea-Weed	8.25	96.00
" Van Deusen's Mandrake	7.75	90.00
Troches, Arnold's Cough	2.00	....
" Brown's Bronchial, small	1.85	21.00
" " " medium	3.75	42.00
" " " large	7.50	84.00

	Doz.	Gross.
Troches, Byram's Tar and W. C.	$1.75	....
" Edey's Carbolic	1.75	....
Vegetine, Stevens	10.00	....
" Powder	4.00	....
Vermifuge, Brown's O. P.	3.75	$41.00
" Fahnestock's B. A.	1.50	17.25
" " B. L.	1.45	15.00
" Jayne's Tonic, small	2.85	....
" " " large	3.80	....
" McLane's	1.50	17.25
" Peery's Dead Shot	1.50	17.50
Water, Cologne, Toilet glass stopped bots., 4 oz. S. R. V. D. & Co	4.00	
" " Toilet glass stopped bottles, 8 oz. S. R. V. D. & Co	6.00	
" " Toilet glass stopped bottles, 16 oz. S. R. V. D. & Co	11.00	
" " Toilet glass stopped bottles, 32 oz. S. R. V. D. & Co	18.00	....
" Florida, Lanman & Kemp's	5.25	62.00
Wine, Pepsin, Boudault's, ½ pints	10.00	...
" " " pints	17.02	....
" Hawley's, ½ pints	6.00	....
" " pints	12.00	....
" Tar, Crooks	7.50	....
Wine of the Woods, trial size	2.00	....
" " " $1.00 size	7.50	....
Zylo-Balsamum, Mrs. Allen's, S. A	6.00	66.00

MINERAL WATERS.

A full line of Domestic and Foreign Mineral Waters in stock, at lowest prices.

DRUGGISTS' SUNDRIES.

Fancy Goods,

Soaps and Perfumery,

Foreign and American Toilet Articles,

Scales,

Trusses,

Instruments,

Etc. Etc. Etc.

DRUGGISTS' GLASSWARE.

The extent and variety of the above lines of goods render a detailed enumeration, for want of space, impossible.

S. R. Van Duzer's

MANUFACTURING DEPARTMENT.

Specialties,

STANDARD PREPARATIONS.

Office of S. R. Van Duzer,

New-York, April, 1880.

To the Trade:

I have the pleasure of presenting you herewith Catalogue of Specialties of my own manufacture, prices and discounts revised to date. I would ask a careful examination of this list. No similar goods, of either foreign or domestic manufacture, surpass them in quality, and each year shows an increase in sales to first-class trade. Liberal terms to the trade, and absolute guarantee of perfect satisfaction in every particular. Sample orders solicited.

Yours, very respectfully,

S. R. Van Duzer,

35 Barclay St. and 40 Park Place, New-York.

Fac-simile of Label and two oz. Bottle.
(Beautiful Lithograph Label.)

PRICE LIST. APRIL, 1880.

S. R. Van Duzer & Co's

FRUIT FLAVORING

EXTRACTS

FOR FLAVORING.

Ice-Cream, Blanc Mange, Jellies, Custards,
Puddings, &c., flavored with these Ex-
tracts are unequaled for richness
and delicacy of flavor.

THEY ARE EXPRESSED FROM SOUND SELECTED FRUITS.

·HEALTHY—BECAUSE PURE.

Cheap—because half the quantity is only required of
these extracts compared with others.

Put up in elegant style, white glass bottles, 1 dozen boxes.
3 sizes: 2 oz., 5 oz. and 10 oz.   Also pints and quarts.

Extract Lemon,
     Peach,
     Orange,
     Almond,
     Nutmeg.
     Celery,
     Nectarine,
     Cinnamon,
     Cloves,
     Jamaica Ginger,
     Raspberry,
     Strawberry,
     Pine-apple,
     Rose,
     Blush.

2 oz. per gro.	*$24.00*
5 oz., per doz.	*4.00*
10 oz., "	*8.00*
Pints, "	*15.50*
Quarts,"	*30.00*
Gall.	*9.50*

Extract Vanilla

2 oz., per gross	*$36.00*
5 oz., per doz	*6.00*
10 oz , "	*12.00*
Pints, "	*22.50*
Quarts, "	*43.00*
Gall.	*13.50*

Discount, 15 per cent.

Quantities one gross.

LUPIN'S

FLAVORING ✦
✦ EXTRACTS.

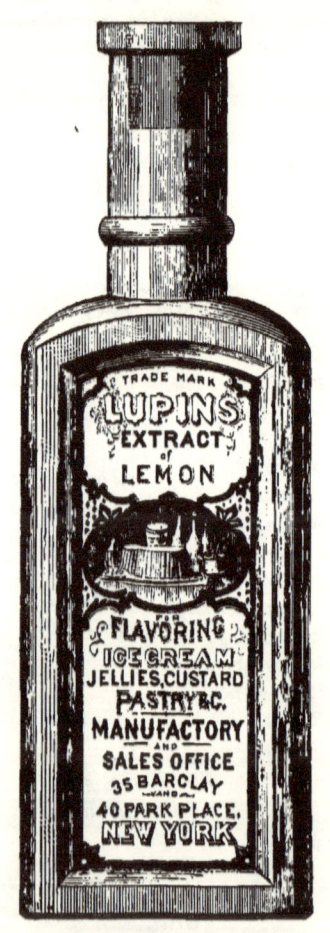

Fac-simile of Bottle and Label.

⚮ LUPIN'S ⚮

FLAVORING ✢
✢ EXTRACTS.

Lupin's Extracts, as you will note below, are offered at a very low price. The quality, of course, is NOT EQUAL to our Fruit Brand, but fully equal to many brands in market selling at higher prices.

Put up in elegant style, white glass bottles, one dozen boxes. Three sizes : 2 oz., 5 oz. and 10 oz. Also, pints and quarts.

Extract Lemon,		
Peach,		
Orange,		
Almond,		
Nutmeg,	2 oz., per gross,	$18.00
Celery,	5 oz., per doz.,	3.00
Nectarine,	10 oz., ``	6.00
Cinnamon,	Pints, ``	11.00
Cloves,	Quarts, ``	21.00
Jamaica Ginger,	Gall.	6.50
Raspberry,		
Strawberry,		
Pine-apple,		
Blush,		
Rose,		

	2 oz., per gross,	$21.00
	5 oz., per doz.,	3.50
Extract Vanilla	10 oz.. ``	7.00
	Pints, ``	13.00
	Quarts, ``	25.00
	Gall.	8.00

Discount, 15 per cent.

Quantities one gross.

⇾ Roland's ⇽

Flavoring ✛ Extracts.

Fac-simile of Bottle and Label.

⇢ Roland's ⇠

Flavoring ⸭ Extracts.

Small Size only.

Put up in White Glass Bottles.   One Doz. Boxes.

Extract Lemon,
 Extract Peach,
  Extract Orange,
   Extract Almond,
    Extract Nutmeg,
     Extract Celery,
      Extract Nectarine,
Extract Cinnamon,
 Extract Cloves,
  Extract Jamaica Ginger,
   Extract Raspberry,
    Extract Strawberry,
     Extract Pine-apple,
     Extract Blush,
      Extract Rose.

Per Gross *$12.00*

Extract Vanilla.

Per Gross *$15.00*

Discount, 15 per cent.

Quantities one gross.

S. R. Van Duzer & Co's

Celebrated Pure

Concentrated Essence ∴

OF

∴ True Jamaica Ginger.

The above Cut represents a fac-simile of our Label and Bottle Wrapper

S. R. Van Duzer & Co's

Celebrated Pure

Conceŋtrated Esseŋce ∴

OF

∴ True Jaɱaica Giŋger.

Packed in One Dozen Packages.

In 4 oz. Bottles.................... ......gross, $36.00
"   "   ....doz.   3.25

PURE Conceŋtrated Esseŋce Jamaica Giŋger, with those who kŋow its many virtues, is held as a household necessity. Its toŋic aŋd correcting influeŋces have ɱade it of priceless value. It is delicious to tḫe taste aŋd eŋtirely harɱless. It canŋot fail to cure Heartburŋ, Sour Stoɱach, Iŋdigestion, Cramps, aŋd Cḫolera Ɱorbus. The eŋormous consumptioŋ of it has offered special inducemeŋts to many to ɱanufacture it froɱ iŋferior root, while otḫers wḫo have, iŋ the past, obtaiŋed a reputatioŋ for their article, are ŋow careless, and palm off aŋ inferior article. The iɱmense demand for our Preparatioŋ ḫas induced us to maŋufacture it on a very exteŋsive scale, aŋd the reliable' quality, perfect purity aŋd excellence of our Preparation sḫall be maintaiŋed.

→Roland's Essence Jamaica Ginger.←

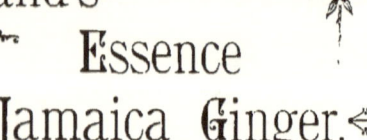

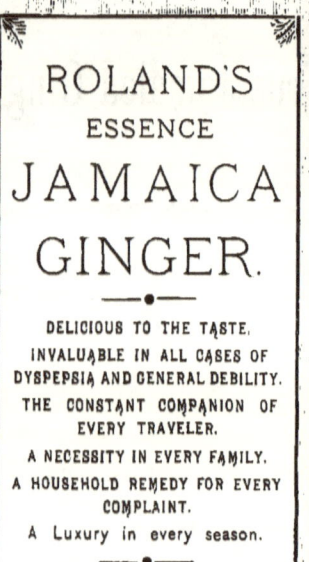

The above cut represents a fac-simile of our Label and Bottle Wrapper.

⇶ Roland's

Essence

Jamaica Ginger. ⇷

✛

Packed in One Dozen Boxes.

In 2 oz. Bottles ....gross, $20.00
"   "   ......doz.   1.75

THE quality and strength of Roland's Essence Ginger is fully equal to any other.

The size of the bottle and the price have been fixed to supply a demand for a bottle that can be retailed for Twenty-five cents.

This article contains all the medicinal properties of the article bearing our own name.

S. R. Van Duzer & Co's

SELECTED

Warranted Pure

→ Ground Spices.

Fac-simile of Cans.
Labels printed in Gold and Green.

S. R. Van Duzer & Co's

Warranted Pure

→Ground Spices.

THESE spices are carefully selected of the very best quality and ground under our own immediate supervision. We Guarantee the Perfect Purity of every package bearing our name.

✛

Packed in New and Attractive Style.
Tin Cans.

✛

Net Prices.

	1 lb. Cans. Per lb.	¼ lb. Cans. Per lb.	¼ lb. Cans. Per lb.	A Cans. Per doz.	B Cans. Per doz.	C Cans. Per doz.
Ginger, African.........	16	18	20	55	45	35
" Jamaica.........	32	34	36	85	65	50
Pepper, Black............	25	27	29	70	55	37
" Red............	30	32	34	65	65	45
" White..........	33	35	37	85	65	45
Allspice.................	28	30	32	75	60	40
Cloves.................	60	62	64	1.30	1.05	75
Cinnamon..............	42	44	46	1.10	85	60
Mace..................	1.06	1.08	1.10	2.50	1.75	1.00
Nutmegs...............	1.06	1.08	1.10	2.50	1.75	1.00

1 lb., ½ lb., and ¼ lb. cans, packed in 12 lb. boxes. A, B and C cans packed in 3 doz. boxes. Ground Spices in Bulk, in Barrels, Kegs and Boxes.

✛

THESE SPICES ARE STRICTLY PURE.

✛

The Trade can rely on our Ground Spices.
We put up only the one quality.

S. R. Van Duzer & Co's

Perfection

⚜Baking, or　⚜

⚜　Yeast Powder.⚜

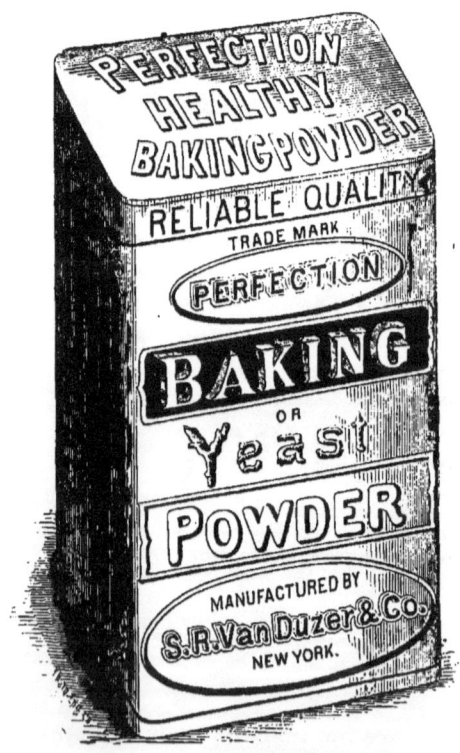

Fac-simile of Cans and Labels, printed in Gold and Drab.

S. R. Van Duzer & Co's

Perfection

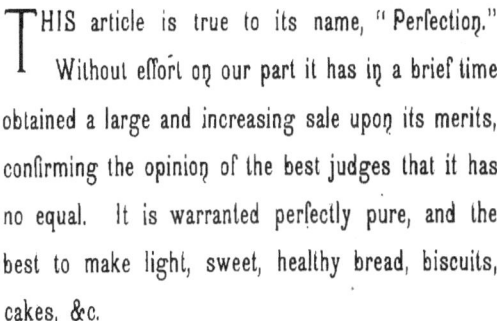

✥Baking, or ✢

✢ Yeast Powder.✥

———✥✷✥———

THIS article is true to its name, "Perfection." Without effort on our part it has in a brief time obtained a large and increasing sale upon its merits, confirming the opinion of the best judges that it has no equal. It is warranted perfectly pure, and the best to make light, sweet, healthy bread, biscuits, cakes, &c.

———✥✷✥———

SQUARE TIN CANS, 2, 3, and 6 doz. Boxes.

		Net Price.
¼ lb. square cans............. ....gross,	$13.20
½ lb. " "	"	24.00
1 lb. " "	"	45.00
5 lb. round cans, hotel and baker's size............lb.	.30
10 lb. " " " " " " .... "	.28

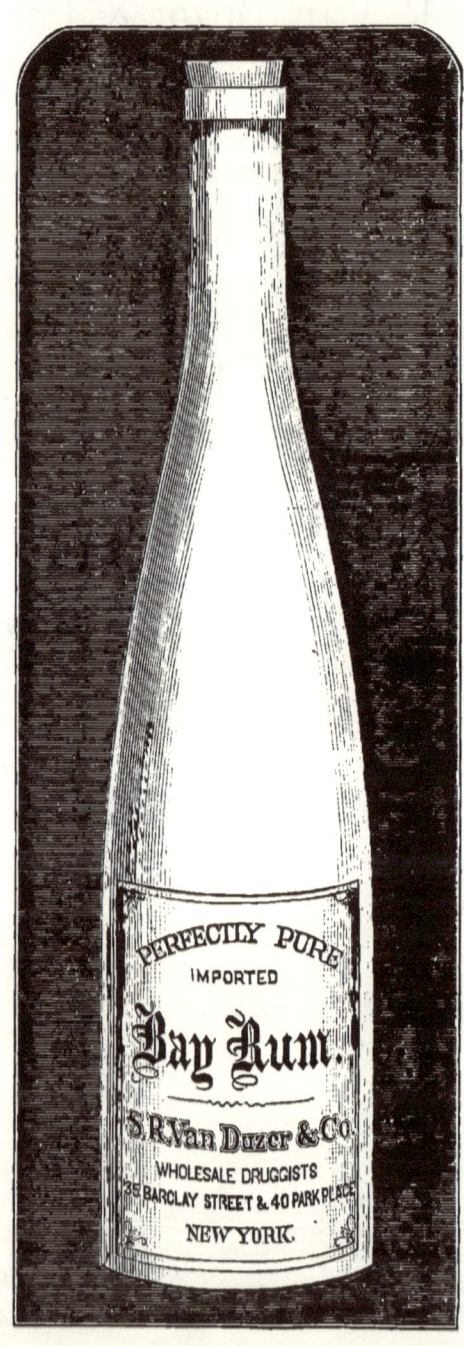

S. R. Van Duzer & Co's

PERFECTLY PURE
IMPORTED

Bay Rum.

Hock bottles, quarts, packed in doz. boxes....doz. $6.75
Hock bottles, pints, packed in doz. boxes..... " 4 50
Hock bottles, ½ pints, packed in 2 doz. boxes, " 3.co

Net Prices.

S. R. Van Duzer & Co's

TOILET

Cologne Water.

Our Cologne Water is fully equal to the best imported.

Toilet glass stopped bottles, 4 oz ... . doz. $4.00
Toilet glass stopped bottles, 8 oz.... " 6 00
Toilet glass stopped bottles, 16 oz .... " 11.00
Toilet glass stopped bottles, 32 oz ...... " 18 00

Net Prices.

S. R. Van Duzer,

Sole Agent for United States.

Floral Bell Fragrant Elixir

OR

Liquid Dentifrice.

Each bottle enclosed in an elegant card-board case.

Trade Prices.

Floral Bell Fragrant Elixir...............gro. $66.00
Floral Bell Fragrant Elixir...............doz. 6.00
Floral Bell Fragrant Elixir...............bottle, 0.75

S. R. Van Duzer,

Sole Agent for United States.

Bridal Bouquet Bloom.

For Beautifying the Complexion.

Each bottle enclosed in an Elegant card-board case.

Trade Prices.

Bridal Bouquet Bloom...... ....gro. $57.00
Bridal Bouquet Bloom....................doz. 5.25
Bridal Bouquet Bloom....................bottle, 0.75

S. R. Van Duzer & Co's

Seidlitz Powders.

Strictly First-Class Material.   ✳

✳   Guaranteed in Every Particular.

	Per Gross.
Full Weight (40 lb. Seidlitz mixture to the gross).....	$33.00
Extra Weight (50 lb. " " ").....	39.00

S. R. Van Duzer & Co's
Special Safety ✢
✢ Friction Matches.

The above is a fac-simile of our Label on each box of our Matches.

TOO MUCH caution cannot be exercised in the selection and use of matches.

The Fire Commissioners of all our large cities, in their reports, say that much loss of life and destruction of dwellings by fire are caused directly by the use of common matches, that are unsafe, made without care, and of inferior quality.

Our Special Safety Friction Matches are commended by the Fire Insurance Companies as the safest and best.

First-class hotels in all parts of the country prefer these to all others.

They have stood the test of years in climates where all others have failed. DAMPNESS does not affect them.

Every box is full count, and every match is selected, and guaranteed that it will ignite when fairly struck ; this fact presents a practical item of economy.

See that the words Special Safety are on every box, together with our name, and take no other ; as inferior matches are often substituted as being "just as good," they are not and cannot be.

One trial will prove the superiority of

S. R. VAN DUZER & CO'S
Special Safety Friction Matches.

$2.50 per gross 100's........ ....packed in 5 and 10 gross cases.
  7.35   "   300's.........   "   3½ gross cases.

Prices Net Cash.

S. R. Van Duzer,

Sole Agent in the United States for this brand Blacking.

FOUR SIZES:

No. 1.............................$2.75 per gross.
" 2.................................... 3.25   "
" 3.................................... 4.00   "
" 4.................................... 5.50   "

Net Prices.

Fac-simile of Label on each box.

Royal Silver Lustre

STOVE  POLISH.

FOR POLISHING STOVES, GRATES, &c.

Warranted equal to Dixon's or any other manufacture.

Price.................. ....$3 50 per gross.

Net Price.

S. R. VAN DUZER & CO'S

Imported Super-Carb. Soda.

Warranted Pure. Our Own Brand.

Per lb.

In 1 lb. papers (36 and 60 lb. boxes) .... 5½c.
In ½ lb. papers (36 and 60 lb. boxes) .... 5¾c.
In ¼ lb. papers (36 and 60 lb. boxes) .... 6¼c.
In ass'd papers (36 and 60 lb. boxes) .... 5¾c.

Net Prices.

✛

S. R. VAN DUZER & CO'S

Perfection Saleratus.

Reliable Quality, Standard Purity, and Excellence.

Per lb.

Pure, in 1 lb. papers (36 and 60 lb. boxes) .... 6 c.
Pure, in ½ lb. papers (36 and 60 lb. boxes) ....:.. 6¼c.
Pure, in ¼ lb. papers (36 and 60 lb. boxes) .... 6¾c.
Pure, in ass'd papers, ¼, ½ and 1 lb., in 36 and 60 lb. bxs. 6¼c.

Net Prices.

✛

S. R. VAN DUZER & CO'S

Liquid Laundry Bluing.

Gross.

In 2 oz. bottles, 3 doz. boxes...................... $3.50
In 4 oz. bottles, 3 doz. boxes...................... 4.75
In 8 oz. bottles, 3 doz. boxes...................... 7.00
In 12 oz. bottles, 3 doz. boxes........:.............. 10.75
In 16 oz. bottles, 1 doz. boxes...................... 14.00
In 32 oz. bottles, 1 doz. boxes...................... 25.00

Net Prices.

✛

S. R. VAN DUZER & CO'S

Dry Laundry Bluing.

Gross.

In boxes, small (pepper-box style, improved tin top).... $2.00
In boxes, large (pepper-box style, improved tin top).... 3.00
In boxes, small (flat box style) ....:.......... 2.25
In boxes, large (flat box style)...................... 3.25

Net Prices.

✛

S. R. VAN DUZER & CO'S

Sewing Machine Oil.

Gross.

In 2 oz. flint bottles................................$10.00

Net Price.

S. R. VAN DUZER & CO'S

PURE MEDICINAL

Cod Liver Oil.

Gross (full size bottles) $66.00
   "   (half   "   ) 36.00

———•———

ROLAND'S

Insect Powder.

Gross $18.00

•———

ROLAND'S

"WINDSOR BRAND"

Benzine.

Gross $9.00

———•———

Olive or Salad Oil.

OUR OWN IMPORTATION.

Bottled Expressly for our Own Trade.

Lucca Olive Oil.

(CALLISTO FRANCESCONI & CO.)

Quarts, 1 doz. cases. . . . . per doz. $7.50
Pints, 2   "   " case, 8.50
½ Pints, 2 "   . . . . " "   5.00
3 gall. tin cans, 4-can cases. . . . . " gall. 2.85

S. R. Van Duzer's

MANUFACTURING DEPARTMENT.

✢ Specialtie). ✢

STANDARD PREPARATIONS.

S. R. VAN DUZER & CO'S
FRUIT FLAVORING EXTRACTS.

LUPIN'S FLAVORING EXTRACTS.

S. R. VAN DUZER & CO'S
PERFECTION SALERATUS.

S. R. VAN DUZER & CO'S
IMPORTED SUPER-CARB. SODA.

S. R. VAN DUZER & CO'S
SELECTED
WARRANTED PURE GROUND SPICES.

S. R. VAN DUZER & CO'S
SPECIAL SAFETY FRICTION MATCHES.

S. R. VAN DUZER & CO'S
LIQUID LAUNDRY BLUING.

S. R. VAN DUZER & CO'S
DRY LAUNDRY BLUING.

S. R. VAN DUZER & CO'S
PURE IMPORTED BAY RUM.

S. R. VAN DUZER & CO'S
TOILET COLOGNE WATER.

S. R. VAN DUZER & CO'S
PERFECTION
BAKING, OR YEAST POWDER.

S. R. VAN DUZER & CO'S
CELEBRATED PURE
CONCENTRATED ESSENCE OF TRUE
JAMAICA GINGER.

S. R. Van Duzer's

MANUFACTURING DEPARTMENT.

✛ Specialties. ✛

STANDARD PREPARATIONS.

S. R. VAN DUZER & CO'S
SEIDLITZ POWDERS.

S. R. VAN DUZER & CO'S
PURE MEDICINAL
COD LIVER OIL.

S. R. VAN DUZER & CO'S
SEWING MACHINE OIL.

S. R. VAN DUZER,
SOLE AGENT
CALLISTO FRANCESCONI & CO.
OLIVE OIL.
BOTTLED EXPRESSLY FOR OUR TRADE.

S. R. VAN DUZER,
SOLE AGENT FOR THE UNITED STATES,
ROYAL BRAND ENGLISH BLACKING.

S. R. VAN DUZER,
SOLE AGENT
SILVER LUSTRE STOVE POLISH.

ROLAND'S
FLAVORING EXTRACTS.

ROLAND'S
ESSENCE JAMAICA GINGER.

ROLAND'S
"WINDSOR BRAND" BENZINE.

ROLAND'S
TRUE PERSIAN
INSECT POWDER.

⇒ Paint and Color Department. ⇐

PRICE LIST.

Terms Net Cash, payable within 30 days, in current funds in New-York, subject to draft if not paid at the expiration of that time. **Prices subject to future changes in market.** We give in List of Sundries two prices; generally, the difference only covers the increased cost of putting up small quantities. Original packages always at the lowest prices.

Office of S. R. Van Duzer.

New-York, April, 1880.

To the Trade.

MY stock consists of a large and most complete assortment of all articles in this line. To explain the quality of the several brands of colors I offer, would say, all colors dry and in oil bearing my own name and labeled Genuine are guaranteed by me to be of absolute purity.

The Royal brand, my second quality, is fully equal to many of the so-called "genuine goods."

The Crown brand, next, at a corresponding reduction in price, supplies the want when cheapness is imperative.

The English Lawn Green, which has become a standard article, I commend for its brilliancy and durability of color as the best blind-green.

Parties who may favor me with their orders, whether for large or small quantities, may be assured of lowest market prices, perfect satisfaction in qualities, and prompt shipment.

Yours, very respectfully,

S. R. Van Duzer,

35 Barclay St. and 40 Park Place, New-York.

WHITE LEAD ✚

AND

✚ WHITE ZINC

IN OIL.

Exclusively my Own Brands.

WHITE LEAD—In Oil.

	25 lb. kegs.	25 lb. cans.	Ass'd cans.
Horse Head Brand......lb.	6½c.	7 c.	8½c.
Gold Seal " "	6	5½	8

Leads of my own brands (25 lb. cans), packed in 100 and 200 lb. cases; assorted cans (1, 2, 3, 4 and 5 lbs.), in 110 lb. cases.

Atlantic Brand....	
Brooklyn "	
Jewett "	} At lowest market rates
English Genuine BB...	

Exclusively my Own Brands.

WHITE ZINC—In Oil.

	25 lb. kegs.	25 lb. cans.	Ass'd cans.
P. & L. Zinc, Equity Brand..lb.	6½c.	7c.	8½c.
French " Gold Seal.....	7½	8	9½
" " Red "	8½	9	
" " Green "	9½	10	

The above are packed as noted under White Lead.

WHITE ZINC—In Varnish.

S. R. V. D. & Co., Genuine Parlor Finish,
1 to 4 lb. cans......... .... lb.   18c.
S. R. V. D. & Co., Gloss Finish, 1 to 4 lb.
cans...... ....lb.   16c.

S. R. Van Duzer's

GENUINE, ROYAL AND CROWN BRANDS

Colors in Oil.

Put up in Cans from 1 lb. to 50 lbs. each, and packed in
Cases to suit Dealers.

A Reduction in Prices when larger than 1 and 2 lb. cans are ordered.

BLACKS--In Oil.

	Genuine.	Royal.	Crown.
Coach Black, Japan......1 & 2 lb. Cans,	$ .22	$ .17	
" " Oil .. ....1 & 2 lb. Cans,	.17	.14	$ .12
Drop " " ....1 & 2 lb. Cans,	.17	.14	.12
Lamp " " ....1 & 2 lb. Cans,	.14	.12	.11
Black Paint, Assorted....1 to 5 lb. Cans,	.14	.11	.10
" ....7, 10 & 14 lb. Cans,	.13	.10	.09
" ....25 & 50 lb. Kegs,	.11	.09	.08

BLUES--In Oil.

Chinese Blue..........½ & 1 lb. Cans,	.37		
Prussian Blue......¼, ½ & 1 lb. Cans,	.32	.26	.22
Ultramarine Blue. .½ & 1 lb. Cans,	.20	.15	
Blue Paint ....1 & 2 lb. Cans,	.13	.11	.10
Barrel Blue... ....In Kegs,	.09		
Celestial.............. ...In Kegs,	.11		

YELLOWS—In Oil.

Chrome Yellow ....1 to 2 lb. Cans,	.20	.15	.14
Oxford Stone Yel., Ass'd.1 to 5 lb. Cans,	.17	.13	.11
Yellow Ochre. ....1 to 5 lb. Cans,	.11	.10	.09
Yellow Ochre. .....25 to 500 lb. Kegs,	.10	.09	.08

GREENS—In Oil.

English Lawn Green, L. M. D., for Window Blinds and Ornamental Iron Work and Machinery. S. R. V. D., Sole Importer. Assorted, 1 to 5 lb. Cans, warranted the most brilliant and permanent green in market..............	.16		
Chrome Green, Assorted, 1 to 5 lb. Cans,	.15	.12	.10
Paris Green, " 1 to 5 lb. Cans,	.20	.17	.14
Hibernia Green, " 1 to 5 lb. Cans,	.15	.12	.10
Imperial Green, " 1 to 5 lb. Cans,	.14	.12	.10
Verdigris Green, " 1 to 5 lb. Cans,	.32	.27	.22

REDS—In Oil.

Vermilion, American.....1 & 2 lb. Cans,	.20	.15	.14
Indian Red ....1 & 2 lb. Cans,	.17	.14	.12
Flat Brick Red. ....7 & 10 lb. Cans,	.12		
Red Lead....... .....1 & 2 lb. Cans,	.12		
Red Paint (Ven. Red), Ass'd.1 to 5 lb. Cans,	.11	.10	.09
Red Paint, " Assd. 25 to 500 lb. Kegs,	.10	.09	.08

S. R. Van Duzer's

GENUINE, ROYAL AND CROWN BRANDS

Colors in Oil.

Put up in Cans from 1 lb. to 50 lbs. each, and packed in
Cases to suit Dealers.

A Reduction in Prices when larger than 1 and 2 lb. cans are ordered.

BROWNS—In Oil.

		Gennine.	Royal.	Crown.
Burnt Sienna	1 & 2 lb. Cans,	.15	.11	.09
Raw Sienna	1 & 2 lb. Cans,	.15	.11	.09
Burnt Umber	1 & 2 lb. Cans,	.14	11	09
Raw Umber	1 & 2 lb. Cans,	.14	.11	.09
Van Dyke Brown	1 & 2 lb. Cans,	.15	.11	.09
Spanish Brown	1 & 2 lb. Cans,	.13	11	.09
Metallic Brown	Kegs & Pails,	.09		

PATENT DRYER.

Patent Dryer, Ass'ted	1 to 5 lb. Cans,	.10
Patent Dryer	7, 10, 14 & 25 lb. Cans,	09
Patent Dryer, Eng.	7 & 14 lb. Cans,	.11

DISTEMPER COLORS.

Burnt Sienna	1 lb. Bottles,	.14
Raw Sienna	1 lb. Bottles,	.14
Burnt Umber	1 lb. Bottles,	.14
Raw Umber	1 lb. Bottles,	.14
Van Dyke Brown	1 lb. Bottles,	.14
Drop Black	1 lb. Bottles,	.14
Carmine Lake	1 lb. Bottles,	.42

GRAINING COLORS—
IN OIL.

Light Oak Color	1 to 5 lb. Cans,	.14
Dark Oak Color	1 to 5 lb. Cans,	.14
Walnut Color	1 to 5 lb. Cans,	.14

COPPER PAINT—
FOR VESSELS' BOTTOMS.

Per Gallon 1.75

PUTTY.

Made only with Pure Linseed Oil.

Putty in Bulk, Barrels, Kegs & Tubs		.02½
Putty in Bladders, Bbls. & Half Bbls		.02¾
Putty in Round Cans	12½ lb.	.03¾
Putty in " "	25 lb.	.03
Putty in " "	50 lb.	.03

Cans are packed in 100 & 200 lb. Cases.

S. R. Van Duzer's
GENUINE, ROYAL AND CROWN BRANDS

Colors Dry.

Put up in Cans, Kegs and Barrels.

BLACKS—Dry.

		Genuine.	Royal.	Crown.
Drop Black, English, Ex.	Kegs,	.17	.14	
Drop Black, Eng.. Ex.. Pow'd	Kegs,	.18	.15	
Drop Black, American	Bbls. & Kegs,	.12	.11	
Drop Black, American, Pow'd	Kegs,	.13	.12	
Ivory Black, English	Kegs,	.07		
Ivory Black, American	Kegs,	.05		
Blue Black, English	Kegs,	09		
Frankfort Black, English	Kegs,	27		

BLUES—Dry.

Prussian Blue, Lump	Boxes, 28 lb.	.47	.35	
Prussian Blue, Pow'd	Boxes, 25 lb.	.49	.37	
Chinese Blue, Lump	Boxes, 25 lb.	.57		
Chinese Blue, Pow'd	Boxes, 25 lb.	.59		
Celestial Blue, Pow'd	Kegs, 100 ib.	10		
Ultramarine Blue, Ex.	Boxes, 28 lb.	.22	.12	
Potter's Blue	Kegs,	32		
Refiner's Blue	Kegs,	.60		
Verditer Blue	Kegs,	.27		
Soluble Blue, Pow'd	Boxes, 25 lb.	.65		

BROWNS—Dry.

Sienna, Italian, Raw, Pow'd	Kegs,	.09	.05
Sienna, Italian, Burnt, Pow'd	Kegs,	08	.05
Umber, Turkey, Raw, Pow'd	Kegs,	.05	03
Umber, Turkey, Burnt, Pow'd	Kegs,	.06	.03
Van Dyke Brown, Pow'd	Kegs,	.08	05
Purple Brown, English	Kegs,	.08	

GREENS—Dry.

English Lawn Green, L. M. & D.	.15		
Chrome Green, L. M. & D.	.14	.11	
Hibernia Green	.13	.10	
Paris Green, Iron Cans, 14, 28 & 56 lb.	.25	23	.21
1 lb. tins 1 c., 2 lb. ½ c. advance on above prices.			
American Green	100 lb. Kegs,	.09	
Brunswick Green, L. & D.	100 lb. Kegs,	.07	
Verdigris, French, Pow'd	.45		
Green, English, Bronze	.13		
Green, English, Quaker	.13		
Green, English, Verditer	.27		

YELLOWS—Dry.

Chrome Yellow, L. M. & O	.20	.18	.15
Chrome Yellow, Red	.25	.22	
Chinese Yellow	Kegs and Barrels,	.07½	

REDS—Dry.

English Vermilion, 30 & 50 lb. Bags	.70		
Trieste Vermilion	.75		
Chinese Vermilion	.90		
Turkey Scarlet Vermilion, L. & D., 6 lb. Tins,	.18	.16	
Carmine Nakarat	1 oz. Bottles,	.60	
Carmine No. 40	1 oz. Bottles,	.55	
Victoria Lake	25 lb. Boxes,	.40	
English Rose Lake	25 lb. Boxes,	.25	
Red, Indian	Kegs,	.10	.08
Red, Tuscan	10 lb. Boxes,	.17	
Rose Pink, English	Barrels & Kegs,	.12	

VARNISHES.

STANDARD QUALITY.

✣

Coach Varnish.

	Per Gall.
Wearing Body	$4.00
Coach "	3.50
Carriage or Gearing	3.25
Coach Body, Extra Light	3.00
Hard Drying or Rubbing	3.50
No. 1 Coach, Extra	2.00
No. 1 "	1.75
No. 2 "	1.50

Furniture Varnish.

Polishing, Extra	5.50
" No. 1	5.25
Furniture, Extra	1.50
" No. 1	1.25
" No. 2	1.10

White Varnish.

Damar, Extra Heavy	1.75
" No. 1	1.50
White Enamel	2.50
" Copal	4.00
Picture, Extra Light	5.00

Black Varnish.

Asphaltum or Iron	1.10
Black Leather	4.00
" Baking Japan	1.25
" Enamel	2.50

Spirit Varnishes.

White Shellac Spirits	4.00
Brown " " Extra	3.50
" " " Ordinary	3.00
Light Spirit Varnish	2.00

Dryers.

Japan Gold Size	3.00
" Coach Painters'	1.75
Brown Japan, Windsor	
" " No. 1	.90
Liquid Dryer	.90

Miscellaneous.

Agricultural, No. 1	2.00
" No. 2	1.50
Mastic Gum, Extra	20.00
Grecian	5.00
Rosewood Stain	4.00
Black Walnut Stain	1.25
Oil-cloth	1.75

Special Quotations are given when large quantities are required.

Varnishes put up in any size Cans, also in Barrels and Half Barrels.

S.÷R.÷Van÷Duzer's

"COTTAGE"

READY ∴ MIXED ∴ PAINTS.

PREPARED FOR IMMEDIATE USE, AND GUARANTEED
TO BE PURE.

These are Pure Linseed Oil Paints, and weigh about 15 pounds per gallon.

In One Gallon Cans.

	Per Gallon.
Vermilion	... $3.00
Chrome Yellow	2.75
Permanent Green	2.25
Black	2.00
Light Blue.	2.00
Dark Blue..................	2.00
Pea Green....................	2.00
Lilac.	2.00
White.....	1.50
All other Shades...........	1.50

Also packed in Quart and Half Gallon Cans.

Cases contain.................Ten 1 gal. cans.
" " ....Twenty ½ "
" " ....Forty ¼ "

¼ gallon cans cost 5c. per can additional.

And in 10, 15, 20, 25 and 40 Gallon Kegs and Barrels.

N. B.—These paints do not contain any Alkalies whatever.

In Cans, Assorted, 1 to 5 Lbs.

	Per Pound.
Outside White......	......$ .14
Inside White	.14
Light Drab...........	.14
Dark Drab	.14
Light Lead Color	.14
Dark Lead Color..	.14
Stone Color.	.14
Yellow Stone Color	.14
French Gray.......	.14
Brown	.14
Venetian Red..................	.14
French Ochre.	.14
French Color......	.14
Buff.	.17
Lilac.	.17
Pea Green......	.17
Light Blue.................	.17
Dark Blue..........	.17
Black	.17
Permanent Green............	.20
Chrome Yellow........	.24
Vermilion	.27

SAMPLE CARDS representing **SHADES** will be furnished
upon application.

BRUSHES,

EVERY SIZE AND FOR EVERY PURPOSE.

Unsurpassed for Quality and Price.

EXTRA GROUND PAINT BRUSHES.

Price	$35.00	40.00	46.00
No	4-0	5-0	6-0

SUPER EXTRA PAINT BRUSHES.

Price	$27.00	31.00	37.00
No	4-0	5-0	6-0

SUPER PAINT BRUSHES.

Price	$8.00	10.50	12.50	14.50	16.00	18.00	20.50
No	1-0	2-0	3-0	4-0	5-0	6-0	7-0

EXTRA P. B. GLOSS PAINT BRUSHES.

Price	$19.50	23.50	29.00	34.00
No	4-0	5-0	6-0	7-0

H. PAINT BRUSHES.

Price	$2.00	2.35	3.00	4.00	4.25	5.00
No	6	5	4	3	2	1
Price	$6.00	6.50	7.50	9.00	10.00	11.50	12.75
No	1-0	2-0	3-0	4-0	5-0	6-0	7-0

P. B. GLOSS PAINT BRUSHES.

Price	$10.15	12.25	16.00	17.75	21.75	25.00	30.50	36.75
No	1-0	2-0	3-0	4-0	5-0	6-0	7-0	8-0

GRAY OVAL PAINT BRUSHES.

Price	$1.85	2.15	2.35	2.85	3.20	3.60
No	6	5	4	3	2	1
Price	$4.30	5.35	6.05	7.10	8.55	14.30	17.10
No	1-0	2-0	3-0	4-0	5-0	6-0	7-0

⟨G⟩ VARNISH BRUSHES.

Price	$2.25	3.00	3.50	4.25	4.75	6.25
No	6	5	4	3	2	1
Price	$7.75	9.75	11.75	12.75	14.50	16.00	17.75
No	1-0	2-0	3-0	4-0	5-0	6-0	7-0

GILT EDGE OVAL VARNISH BRUSHES.

Price	$2.50	3.25	4.25	4.70	5.75	6.50
No	6	5	4	3	2	1
Price	$8.50	10.00	12.25	13.50	15.75	17.75	21.50
No	1-0	2-0	3-0	4-0	5-0	6-0	7-0

Discount on above Line Brushes, 50 per cent.

Prices are per dozen.

BRUSHES,

EVERY SIZE AND FOR EVERY PURPOSE.

Unsurpassed for Quality and Price.

SASH TOOLS.
Extra.

Price	$0.85	1.10	1.30	1.50	1.90	2.00	2.35	2.75	3.25	3.50
No....	1	2	3	4	5	6	7	8	9	10

French.

Price	$1.80	2.00	2.65	3.00	3.65	4.25	4.75	5.50	7.25	8.00
No..	1	2	3	4	5	6	7	8	9	10

WALL PAINT BRUSHES. Quality A.

Price	$8.00	11.00	16.00	17.75
No	1	2	3	4
Inches	3½	4	4½	5

H. PAINTERS' DUSTERS.

Price	$5.00	6.00	7.00	8.00
No...	1	2	3	4

KALSOMINE BRUSHES.
Russia.

Price	$27.80	37.00	49.50
No....	6	7	8

M. x B.

Price	$18.00	22.50	27.00
No..	6	7	8

WHITEWASH BRUSHES.
Ordinary.

Price	$6.25	7.25	9.25	11.50	12.75	16.50	19.50
No	4	5	6	7	8	9	10
Inches	6	6½	7	7½	8½	8¾	9½

C. M.

Price	$6.50	7.25	8.50	9.50	11.50	12.50	14.25
No...	2	4	6	8	10	12	14
Inches	6	6½	7	7½	8	8½	9

WHITEWASH HEADS.
Super.

Price	$19.00	24.00	29.25
No...	8	9	10
Inches	7½	8	8½

Extra C. M.

Price	$10.25	11.25	12.25	14.25	16.75
No	1	2	3	4	5
Inches	6½	7	7½	8¼	8¾

A. x B. WHITEWASH HEADS.

Price	$3.50	4.00	5.00	5.25	6.25	7.25	8.25	10.00	11.50
No	4	5	6	7	8	9	10	11	12
Inches ..	5	5½	6¼	6¾	7½	7¾	8¼	9	9½

GRAY WHITEWASH HEADS.

Price	$4.00	5.75	9.00	11.50	12.75
No	1-0	2-0	3-0	4-0	5-0
Inches ..	6½	7½	8½	9	9

Discount on above Line Brushes, 50 per cent.

Prices are per dozen.

IMPORTED AND DOMESTIC

✢ Colors and Sundries. ✢

— ⟶ ✳ ⟵ —

Alum, Lump..	......bbls. or less, per lb.	$ .02¼	$ 05
" Ground	" "	.02½	05
Axle Grease	......per gross.	9.00	
Bath Brick	......per 100,	3.00	
" " 24 in box.............	. " box,	.75	
Borax...........	....per lb.	.13	15
Brimstone, Roll..........	bbls. or less, per lb.	.02½	.04
Chalk, white, Lump........ "	" "	.00½	.03
" " Prepared Drops.....	"	.06	.08
" " French, Powdered.	"	.06	10
" Red, Lump..	"	.05	07
" " Fingers	"	.06	.08

			dozen.
Chamois Skins, X. P .... kip, 30 skins, per kip,		21.00	8.50
" " P....... " " "		18.00	8.00
" " No. 1. " " "		17.00	7.50
" " " 2.... " " "		15.00	7.00
" " " 3. " " "		14.00	6.50
" " " 4. " " "		13.00	6.00
" " A. " " "		12.00	5 50
" " B. ... " " "		10.00	5.00
" " C....... " " "		9.00	4.50
" " D......... " " "		8.00	4.00
" " E..... " " "		7.00	3 50
" " F......... " " "		6.00	3.00
" " G........ " " "		5.00	2.50
" " XX ..... " " "		9.00	4.50
" " French " " "		18.00	8.00
" Oil Dressed, A... " " "		12.50	5.50
" " B... " " "		11.50	5.25
" " C... " " "		10.50	5.00
" " D... " " "		9.50	4.75
" " E... " " "		8.50	4.50
" " F... " " "		7.50	4.00
China Clay, Super Eng., ½ ton casks....per ton,		18.00	
Copperas..................bbls. or less, per lb.		.01¼	.03
Crayons, Chalk, White. ....per gross,		.14	
Crocus Martis, Eng......... ......per lb.		.12	.15
Dutch Pink .... "		.12	.15
Emery, Pure Turkey, Flour.. ..... "		.06	.08
" " " Grain ...... "		.07	10
" Cloth......... ......per ream,		18.00	
" Paper. ...... "		6.25	
Fillings, American...... ... per lb.		.06	.08
" English........ "		.08	.10
Frostings, White........... .... "		.40	
" Blue, Green, and Purple.. "		.80	
" Canary .... "		1.35	
" Ruby .... "		2.75	
Glaziers' Diamonds, Plain ... .per doz.		30.00	
" " Keyed ... "		36 00	

IMPORTED AND DOMESTIC

✛ Colors and Sundries. ✛

—◄═►·✳·◄═►·—

Glaziers' Points, No. 0, 1, 2, 3 . . . . ⎫
Triangles and Sharps, in boxes of 100 ⎬ per box $6.75
    ½ lb. papers . . . . ⎭

Glue, A . . . . Bbls. or less, per lb., $				.14	.16
"	AA	"	"	"	.18	.20
"	AAA	"	"	"	.25	.27
"	Cooper's A Extra	"	"	"	.32	.35
"	"	1	"	"	"	"	.28	.30
"	"	No. 1	"	"	"	.24	.26
"	"	" IX	"	"	"	.20	.22
"	"	" 1¼ . . .	"	"	"	.17	.19
"	"	" 1⅜ . . .	"	"	"	.16	.18
"	"	" 1½ . . .	"	"	"	.15	.17
"	"	" 1⅝ . . .	"	"	"	.13	.15
"	"	" 1¾ . . .	"	"	"	.12	.14
"	"	" 2	"	"	"	.11	.13 ·
"	"	" 2⅛ . . .	"	"	"	.
"	"	" 2¼ . . .	"	"	"	

Less 5 % in quantities by the barrel.

Gold Leaf, Extra Deep . . . . per pack, $7.25				$7.50
"	"	Usual "	. . . . "	6.75	7.00
"	"	Pale . . . . "	6.50	6.75
Gum, Asphaltum . . . . per lb.,			.10	.12
"	Copal	. . . . "	.40	.45
"	Damar . . . . "	.35	.40
"	Gamboge . . . . "	.70	.75
"	Shellac, Bleached . . . . "	.50	.55
"	"	Campbell's, D. C. . . . . "	.50	.55
"	"	English, No. 1 . . . . "	.45	.50
"	"	" No. 2 . . . . "	.40	.45
"	"	Garnet . . . . "	.40	.45
Indigo, Bengal . . . . "			1 75	1.85
"	Caracas . . . . "	1.20	1.25
"	Manilla, Extra . . . . "	1.10	1.15
"	"	A . . . . "	1.00	1.05

					Black.	Col'd.
Japanned Tins, or iron, 10×14 . . . . per doz.,					$1.75	$2.00
"	"	"	12×17	"	3.50	4.00
"	"	"	14×20 . . .	"	4.50	5.00
"	"	"	18×24	"	7.00	8.00
"	"	"	20×28	"	14.00	16.00
"	"	"	24×36	"	20.00	23.00
"	"	"	28×56	"	30.00	38.00
Knives, Gilders' . . . . per doz., 4.50					
"	Mixing	"	9.50
"	Hack	"	2.50
"	Palette	"	2.75
"	Putty	"	2.50

✛ Colors and Sundries. ✛

LAMP-BLACKS.

Titus, Eddy & Sons,			
Pounds and Assorted...bbls. or less, per lb.		$ .20	$ .22
L. Martins & Co.,			
Ex. Coach Painters, 16 oz. Pap's, { bbls. or less, per lb.		15½	17½
" ½ Pounds.... " "		.17	.19
" ¼ " " "		.19	.21
" Assorted..... " "		.17	.19
Coach Painters, 16 oz. Papers.... " "		.13½	.15½
" ½ Pounds....... " "		.15	.17
" ¼ " " "		17	.19
" Assorted........ " "		.15	.17
Germantown, 16 oz. Papers. " "		.09	.11
" ½ Pounds..... " "		10	.12
" ¼ " " "		.12	.14
" Assorted........ " "		.10	.12
Ordinary (sold by count), Whole Pap's, " "		.03	.05
" " Asst'd " " "		.03	.05
" " ½ " " "		.04	.06
" " ¼ " " "		.05	.07
Double Refined Velvet, in Bulk " "		.10	.12
Germantown " " " "		.07	.09
Super No. 1 " " " "		.06	.08
" " 3 " " " "		.04½	.06½
Cape Cod Lamp-Black, in Fingers, bbls. or less,			
per 100............		.50	1.00
Lead, Black, East India Lump.........per lb.		.07	.09
" " " "Powdered.... "		.08	.10
" " German............. "		.06	.08
" " American.......... "		.04	.06
" Red " ....Kegs or less, "		.07¾	.10
" " English..... " " "		.09½	.12
" White Atlantic Dry. " " "		.08½	.10
" " Horse Hend " " " "		.06½	.08
" " English " " " "		.09½	.12
Litharge, American....... " " "		.07¾	.10
" English. .... " " "		.09¾	.12
Manganese, Black Oxide, Extra .. .... "		.06	.08
" " " Super....... "		.04	.06
Marble Dust........... .....bbls., per bbl.		1.25	

MINERAL PAINTS.

Brandon, Yellow........bbls. or less, per lb.		.01¼	.03
" Roofing.... ... " " "		.01¼	.03
" Red Brown.... " " "		.01¼	.03
Spanish Brown.......... " " "		.01	.02
S. R. V. D. & Co., Metallic, " " "		.01½	.03
Prince Bros. "Ironore" " " "		.01½	.03
Grafton Chocolate Paint.. " " "		.01	.02
" Slate " .. " " "		.01	.02
Ochre, French, Rochelle.. " " "		.01½	.03
" " Havre.... " " "			
" American···. ... " " "		.01	.02
" Washed Dutch.... " " "		.08	.10

IMPORTED AND DOMESTIC

✦ Colors and Sundries. ✦

—·{⟩⟩·✳·⟨⟨·⟩·——

Ochre, English, Oxford, Nat'l Lump....per lb., $	10 $	12
" " " " Pow'd.. "	11	.13
Orange Mineral, English....... "	.10	12
Plaster, Calcined.............bbls., per bbl.,	1.25	
" Dentists'....... .... " "	1.50	
Potash, 1st sorts.......Casks, or less, per lb.,	.05½	.07
Pumice Stone, Selected.......... ..... "	.05	.07
" " Powdered .... "	.04	.06
Rotten " Selected .... "	.08	.10
" " Powdered .... "	.06	.08
Rubbing " English................. "	.08	.10
Red, Eng. Venetian, S. R. V. D. & Co.{ bbls. or less, per lb., }	.01½	.03
" " " H. R. & Co.... " "	.01¾	.03
" " " Cookson's...... " "	.01½	.03
" American Venetian.......... " "	.01¼	.03
Sand Paper, Flint............. .... Ream,	4.50	
" " Eagle.................. "	3.25	
Sea Sand.. .... bbls., per bbl.,	1.25	
Silver Leaf.... ....per pack,	2.00	
Smalts, German Cobalt, Blue, Fine....per lb.,	.15	.17
" " " " Coarse.. "	.15	.17
" American Blue............. "	.10	.12
" Black Superfine .... "	.07	.08
" " Fine... .... "	.06	.07
" " Extra .... "	.04	.05
" Brown .... "	.07	.08
" Maroon ... . "	.07	.08
" Chrome Green.......... "	.07	.08
" Paris " . ... "	.11	.12
" Vermilion.................. "	.11	.12
Sponges, Florida, S. W., Selected.... "	2.50	
" " Carriage .... "	1.00	
" Bahama " .... "	1.25	
Sulphur, Flour of... ...... bbls., "	.03¾	.05
Wax, Pure White.............. ..... "	50	.55
" Refined Yellow. .... "	.28	.30
White, Paris, Imp. Queensgate,{ Casks and bbls. or less, per lb. }	.02¼	.03
" " " Kiln-dried & Bolted " "	.02½	.04
" " " Cliffstone... ...... " "	.01¾	.03
" " " Kiln-dried & Bolted " "	.02	.03
Whiting, Gilder's .... " "	40/100	.02
" " Kiln-dried and Bolted " "	.01	.02
" Commercial........... " "	70/100	.02
" " Kiln-dried & Bolted " "	80/100	.02
Zinc, American, Snow White,{ bbls. or less, per lb., }	.05¾	.08
" " Super....... " " .	.05½	.07
" French, Red Seal..... " "	.08½	.10
" " Green Seal.... " "	.10	.12
" Sulphate .... " "	.06	.08

FRENCH WINDOW GLASS.

SIZES.	SINGLE.				DOUBLE.			
	1	2	3	4	1	2	3	4
6x 8 to 10x15	8.00	6.75	6.25	5.75	12.00	11.00	10.00	9.25
11x14 to 16x24	8.75	8.00	7.50	7.00	14.75	13.75	12.75	11.75
18x22 to 20x30	11.25	10.50	9.75	8.75	19.00	17.75	16.00	
15x36 to 24x30	12.75	11.50	10.00		21.50	19.25	16.50	
26x28 to 24x36	13.50	12.25	11.25		23.00	20.75	18.25	
26x36 to 26x44	14.75	13.75	11.75		25.00	23.00	19.25	
28x46 to 30x50	16.25	15.00	13.00		27.00	25.00	21.25	
30x52 to 30x54	17.25	16.00	13.50		28.50	26.00	22.25	
30x56 to 34x56	18.75	16.75	15.00		30.00	27.75	24.75	
34x58 to 34x60	19.50	18.00	16.00		31.75	30.00	27.00	
36x60 to 40x60	21.00	19.50	18.00		35.50	32.50	30.25	

Sizes above 100 inches—$10 per box extra for every 5 inches.

All sizes over 52 inches in length, and not making 81 united inches, will be charged in 84 united inches bracket.

An additional 10 per cent. will be charged for all Glass more than 40 inches wide.

DISCOUNT,

AMERICAN WINDOW GLASS.

SIZES.	SINGLE.				DOUBLE.			
	1	2	3	4	1	2	3	4
6x 8 to 10x15	8.25	7.50	7.00	6.50	12.75	11.75	10.75	10.00
11x14 to 15x24	9.25	8.50	8.00	7.25	14.50	13.25	12.50	11.25
16x24 to 20x28	10.75	9.75	8.75	7.75	17.25	15.75	14.00	
15x34 to 24x30	12.25	10.75	9.00	8.50	19.75	17.25	14.50	
26x28 to 24x36	13.00	11.50	9.75	9.00	21.00	18.50	15.75	
26x36 to 26x44	14.50	13.25	10.75	9.50	23.25	21.25	17.25	
26x46 to 30x50	15.00	14.00	11.25	10.50	24.00	22.50	18.00	
30x52 to 30x54	16.00	14.50	12.00		25.75	23.25	19.25	
30x56 to 34x56	17.25	15.50	13.50		27.75	25.00	21.75	
34x58 to 34x60	18.25	17.25	15.00		29.25	27.75	24.00	
36x60 to 40x60	20.75	18.75	17.25		33.25	30.00	27.75	

Sizes above 100 inches—$10 per box extra for every 5 inches.

All sizes over 52 inches in length, and not making 81 united inches, will be charged in 84 united inches bracket.

An additional 10 per cent. will be charged for all Glass more than 40 inches wide.

DISCOUNT,

OILS.—Perfectly Pure.

Quotations not binding in case of change in market value.

Linseed Oil, Raw. ...At lowest market rates.
Linseed Oil, Boiled...   "   "   "
Sperm Oil, Bleached..Gall.$1.30   1.35..By Bbl., Gall.$1.25
Elephant Oil, Bleached, "   0.80   0.85..By Bbl., "   0.75
Lard Oil, Prime...... "   0.70   0.75..By Bbl., "   0.65
Lard Oil, No. 1....... "   0.68   0.73..By Bbl., "   0.63
Whale Oil, Bleached.. "   0.70   0.75..By Bbl., "   0.65
Neatsfoot Oil, Extra.. "   0.85   0.90..By Bbl., "   0.75
Neatsfoot Oil, Cooper's "   1.05   1.10..By Bbl., "   0.95
Machine Oil, Extra... "   0.70   0.75..By Bbl., "   0.65
Machine Oil, No. 1... "   0.45   0.50..By Bbl., "   0.40
Strait's Oil.......... "   0.52   0.57..By Bbl., "   0.47
Bank Oil........... "   0.50   0.55. By Bbl., "   0.45
Superior Prime White Coal Oil... ....At lowest market rates.
Spirits Turpentine.............. ..   "   "   "

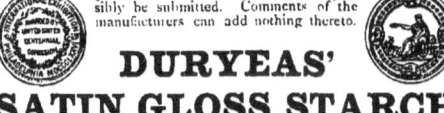

JOHNSTON'S

Patent Standard

DRY SIZED

KALSOMINE.

"Ready For Use."

This Kalsomine is an article that, in the most inexperienced hands, cannot fail to produce a pleasing effect.

It is endorsed by Painters, Dealers and House-keepers, wherever tried.

It is ready for use by the addition of water only, being an impalpable powder.

It will not rub or scale from the wall.

It will work well upon absorbent, or what are known as hot walls.

It is invaluable in cleansing and disinfecting walls that are impregnated with germs of disease.

It is made of the purest white, and in gradations of all the leading and fashionable tints—"from grave to gay, from common to sublime."

It is sold from sample card; all the tints, shades, and colors are warranted in every respect accurate.

It will KEEP FOR YEARS without change in Quality or Color.

It is packed in strong Manilla paper packages, of box form, holding six pounds, with full directions for use.

A six-pound package will cover 400 square feet with one coat, on a hard-finished wall.

A pail of this Kalsomine can be mixed in five minutes.

SEND FOR SAMPLE CARD AND PRICES.

CAUTION.—The wide-spread popularity of my PATENT KALSOMINE and Fresco Paints having induced unscrupulous parties to foist upon the market worthless preparations, under various names, purporting to be for the same purposes, I caution the public to guard against such frauds, by seeing that my Name and Trade-Mark are on every package.

II. M. JOHNSTON, Patentee.

Trade supplied at lowest manufacturers' prices by
S. R. VAN DUZER.

MALTINE.

BY PROF. JOHN ATTFIELD, F. C. S.,

Professor of Practical Chemistry to the Pharmaceutical Society of Great Britain ; Author of a Manual of General Medical and Pharmaceutical Chemistry.

LONDON, 17 BLOOMSBURY SQUARE, W. C., }
October 28th, 1878. }

To Messrs. Reed & Carnrick :

GENTLEMEN :—I have analyzed the extract of malted Wheat, malted Oats, and malted Barley, which you term MALTINE. I have also prepared, myself, some extract from these three malted cereals, and have similarly analyzed it, and may state at once that it corresponds in every respect with the Maltine made by myself. As regards the various Malt Extracts in the market, I may remark that your MALTINE belongs to the non-alcoholic class, and is far richer, not only in the directly nutritious materials, but in the farina digesting Diastase. In comparison, your MALTINE is about ten times as valuable, as a flesh former ; from five to ten times as valuable as a heat producer ; and at least five times as valuable as a starch digesting agent. It contains, unimpaired and in a highly concentrated form, the whole of the valuable materials which it is possible to extract from either malted Wheat, malted Oats or malted Barley.

Yours faithfully,

JOHN ATTFIELD.

List of Maltine Preparations.

MALTINE—Plain.
MALTINE with **Alteratives**. .
MALTINE with **Beef and Iron**.
MALTINE with **Cod Liver Oil and Pancreatine**.
MALTINE with **Cod Liver Oil and Phosphates**.
MALTINE with **Hops**.
MALTINE with **Hypophosphites**.
MALTINE with **Pepsin and Pancreatine**.
MALTINE with **Phosphates**.
MALTINE with **Phos. Iron, Quinia and Strychnia**.
MALTINE Ferrated.
MALTINE WINE.
MALTINE WINE with **Pepsin and Pancreatine**.
MALTINE with **Peptones**.
MALTO-YERBINE.

MALTINE is now in the hands of the Wholesale Trade throughout the United States.

We guarantee that MALTINE *will keep perfectly in any climate, or any season of the year.*

We Manufacture a Full Line of

FLUID EXTRACTS,
Gelatine and Sugar-Coated Pills,
ELIXIRS, &c.

Which we guarantee to be perfect in every respect.

Faithfully yours,

REED & CARNRICK, New-York.

All of the above, and a full line of REED & CARNRICK's other Standard Preparations, supplied to the trade at lowest manufacturers' prices, by

S. R. VAN DUZER.

TEFFT, ✢

GRISWOLD

✢ & CO.

Importers and Jobbers of

DRY

GOODS,

326, 328 & 330 Broadway,

Between Worth and Pearl Sts.

NEW-YORK.

E. T. TEFFT.	
W. E. TEFFT.	G. L. PUTNAM.
J. H. WELLER.	H. R. CLARKE.
G. G. KELLOGG.	G. C. CLARKE.

AUSTIN, NICHOLS & CO.

Importers

AND

Wholesale Grocers,

ALSO

Dealers in Fish

AND

FOREIGN FRUITS

Nos. 106, 108 & 110 Reade St.

NEW-YORK.

✢

Price List Sent on Application.

✢

WILL REMOVE

On or about May 1st, to

American Express Building,

Corner Hudson and Jay Streets.

NATH'L ✛

FISHER

✛ & CO.

Wholesale Dealers in

BOOTS, SHOES

AND RUBBERS,

27 Murray and 31 Warren Sts.

New-York.

NATH'L FISHER.
HENRY DIX.
WM. A. FERRIS.

GEO. W. DAVIS.
IRVING R. FISHER.

EARLY & LANE,

WHOLESALE DEALERS IN

Wood Ware, Cordage,

BROOMS, BRUSHES, MATCHES,
TWINE, BASKETS, ETC.

AND IMPORTERS AND JOBBERS OF

Crockery, China,

Lamps,

AND

Glassware,

145 CHAMBERS STREET,

127 READE STREET,

5 HUDSON STREET,

NEW-YORK.

QUACKENBUSH,

TOWNSEND

✥ # & CO. ✥

Manufacturers and Wholesale Dealers in

HARDWARE.

— ✦ —

Depot for
Wide-Awake Axes,
Rough-and-Ready and Clipper Scythes,
Beaver Files
And Challenge Door and Gate Springs.

— ✦ —

Agents for
NORWICH LOCK MFG. CO.

— ✦ —

85 CHAMBERS & 67 READE STS.

New-York.

HOLBROOK ∴

∴ BROTHERS,

AMERICAN PLATE GLASS,

Sole Agents for the East

OF THE

Crystal Plate Glass Co.

Of St. Louis, Mo.

QUALITY GUARANTEED EQUAL TO THE BEST IMPORTED.

Also, Importers of

French and English

Plate & Window Glass.

ORNAMENTAL GLASS

For Offices, Prescription Cases, Vestibules, &c.

GLAZIERS' DIAMONDS.

---

87 AND 89 BEEKMAN STREET,

AND

53 AND 55 CLIFF STREET,

NEW-YORK.

Trade supplied at Importers' lowest prices, by
S. R. VAN DUZER.

E. Greenfield's Son & Co.

Manufacturers of

CONFECTIONERY,

44 Barclay Street,

NEW-YORK.

✢

**Druggists' Gum Drops.   Licorice Drops.
Cough Drops.   Hoarhound Drops.**

✢

CHOCOLATE CREAM DROPS,
MARSHMALLOW DROPS,
MIXED CANDIES, ETC., ETC.

✢

*All Kinds of Medicated Lozenges
for Druggists' use.*

✢

COLTSFOOT ROCK.
ROCK CANDY, etc.

Trade supplied at manufacturers' lowest prices, by
S. R. VAN DUZER.

S. F. ENGS.   GEO. ENGS.   H. SNYDER, Jr.

P. W. ENGS & SONS,

Wine Merchants,

No. 131 Front Street,

NEW-YORK,

DEALERS IN

SPIRITS AND WINES,

**Importing them from the best
houses abroad,**

Offer to the Drug trade a stock, for variety and excellence unsurpassed by any house in the United States. Druggists who wish to handle

Pure Goods

Are invited to buy of us. We know our stock is as large, if not larger, than any house in the trade, and challenge comparison both in quality and prices.

BOURBON & RYE WHISKIES,

From the best makers,

ALWAYS IN STOCK, "OF ALL AGES."

SAMPLES SENT CARRIAGE FREE.

**Trade supplied at Importers' lowest prices, by
S. R. VAN DUZER.**

DAVID S. BROWN & CO.

Established 1808.

MANUFACTURE THE

Finest and Largest Line of

TOILET SOAPS

In the Country.

ALSO A FINE LINE OF

Toilet Waters

AND

HANDKERCHIEF EXTRACTS

Sold by all Wholesale Druggists and
Notion Jobbers.

———

Trade supplied at manufacturers' lowest prices, by
S. R. VAN DUZER.

"Sweet Bye-and-Bye."

The Odor is Rich and very Lasting.

It has the
LARGEST SALE
of any
Perfume in the
country.

Sold on its honest
merit.

"OUR ROSE BUD,"
"GYPSY MAID,"

Popular Perfumes.

Our **BULK** and **TRIPLE EXTRACTS**
are **Standard.**

CORNING & TAPPAN,

Perfumers,

NEW-YORK.

All of the above, and a full line of Corning & Tappan's other Standard Perfumes, supplied to the trade at lowest manufacturers' prices by

S. R. VAN DUZER.

John Jewett & Sons,

CORRODERS OF LEAD

AND

Crushers of Linseed

This is the ONLY QUALITY of WHITE
LEAD that we have made for the
last twenty-two years.

✠

PACKAGES.

Wood Pails, 12½, 25 and 50 lbs. each.
Kegs,   - - - 100 " "
Casks, about 200, 300, 500 and 600 lbs. each.
Cases containing four 25 lb. tin pails.
  "   "   eight 12½" "
  "   "   100 lbs. ass'd, 1, 2, 3 and 5
          lb. cans.

JOHN JEWETT & SONS,

181 Front Street, New-York.

www.ingramcontent.com/pod-product-compliance
Lightning Source LLC
Chambersburg PA
CBHW020808020726
47495CB00008B/2628